LATE NIGHT LICK VOL 1 PRESENTS LUST, FEAR, & FIRE

A NOVEL

BY NENE CAPRI

Late Night Lick: Lust, Fear, & Fire is a work of fiction. Names,
characters, places, and incidents either are products of the author's
imagination or are used fictitiously, and any resemblance to actual persons,
living or dead, business establishments, events, or locales are entirely
coincidental.

Cover Design: by Lashonda Johnson & Nene Capri
NeneCapri@gmail.com
& Ghostwriterinc2016@gmail.com

Book Interior Design by Lashonda Johnson
Ghostwriterinc2016@gmail.com

Party 4 Two

"Look don't start your shit." Mason said a little above a whisper as Erica's one hundred and one questions had now began to ruin his whole mood.

Don't start your shit. We would have been inside if we left when I said to," Erica spat back.

Mason started to say something to make her mood just as heated as his was about to be. Instead he just looked down at her pouty lips and gazed into her soft brown eyes a peace came over his soul. He just took her hand into his and brought it to his mouth.

"Baby you are absolutely right. We need this weekend. You deserve this." He kissed her hand once more. Whatever you want. You will get." He smiled to seal the deal.

Erica looked up at Mason, his light skin and perfect wavy hair took her back to the day she fell in love with him. However, everything about him had changed, except his looks. He was now her six-foot one, daily reminder of why she should have walked away years ago. But, she put their long history together above her need, to actually be happy. Erica's only hope was that their little vacation would somehow cover the wounds they were both now carrying.

"Thank you, baby." Erica tried to ease Mason's mind.

"Let's just try to have a good time." He pulled her slender frame into his arms and hugged her tightly then whispered in her ear. "No matter what comes our way. I will love you forever and a day."

Erica formed a smile as she played back the way he said that same line right before giving her his name. She closed her eyes and just lived in the moment.

"Your table is ready?" The hostess interrupted them, then lead them through the crowded room to a table right in the middle of the action. "Here you go." She handed them two drink menus. "Your waitress will be right over." She announced loudly competing with the music then walked off.

Mason pulled out her chair, then took the seat next to her. Erica and Mason sat having a visual paradise as their eyes danced from one end of the dancehall to the other. It was the infamous Brazilian Carnival weekend and the scantily dressed woman in costumes and head dress. There were lights and sounds coming from every direction. They sat taking it all in as their senses went into overdrive.

"I'm about to try something I never tried before." Erica did a little shuffle in her seat.

"Get whatever you want baby. Let's just live." He reached over and brought her face to his and began sucking her lips.

Erica's whole face light up as Mason's hands eased between her legs and over the lips of her pussy. "I love you baby." He mouthed as he pulled back slowly.

"Forever." She confirmed licking her lips to savor every bit of his sweetness.

"Good evening love birds," the tall curvy server said with a huge pearly white smile.

Mason's eyes roamed up the slit in her wrap skit to the knot at her waist which was tiny and accented by a double diamond barbell on her navel. His eyes travelled up her breasts and landed again on the smile. His face formed a nervous smirk as his heart beat against his chest.

"Whatever she wants to order," he responded as he forced his eyes back in Erica's direction.

Erica also smiled as she pointed to a few drinks then asked the server to explain which one tasted the best. After a few suggestions she chose two of the biggest drinks they had. Erica collected the menus and passed them to the amazingly shaped woman and watched her until she was out of her sight.

"You like that don't you?" She giggled as she looked at Mason squirm in his seat.

"She was put together baby." He responded nonchalantly not wanting to arouse any unwanted mood swings.

"Shit. I'm not mad. If I was a man I would want to fuck her too." She said feeling the heat of the night enhance her mood.

"You ain't down." He joked as rubbed his hand over her nipples.

"You never know." She responded quickly wanting to enjoy the flow of moment.

Mason snuggled his nose against her neck and whispered in her ear. The couple continued to pet, play, and fantasize as the highlights of the evening entertained them. It was Brazil and the beautiful woman dancing in G-strings and feathers had them both filled with erotic power.

"Here you go. Please enjoy. Let me know if you need anything else." She placed the huge glass goblets in front of them, then sat a straw in each one.

"Thank you." Mason answered again smiling at all that beauty before him.

The server exchanged the friendly gestor, then left the couple to enjoy their drinks.

Erica was turned on by the way Mason flirted and played. It was a side of him she hadn't seen in years and she was loving it. As Erica sipped her drink her eyes roamed over the crowded night club and attempted to digest all the gorgeous brown skin. The men were various shades of milk chocolate, with dark hair, chiseled sexy frames, and big beautiful white smiles. The women were stacked from head to toe, with perky round breasts and juicy asses that sat up high and were slightly covering their erect nipples. She watched the grinding and swaying waist, which moved to the beat of paradise.

As the warm air eased over their skin; Mason rocked to the heat in the air which was giving him a fuck me vibe that you could not deny. Mason moved closer to Erica and just held her tightly as they both sipped strong drinks and rocked seductively to the music.

****

"Oh my god," Tylinn whispered as Sa'Moo's fingers played between the lips of her pussy as she slowly grinded in front of him.

"Let daddy make this pussy cum." He mouthed as he watched his wife give him a show.

Tylinn was caught up and moving her waist to the music and the knowing rhythm of his fingers.

Sa'moo eased his hand out of her skirt, placed them in his mouth and sucked gently as he locked her in the eyes.

"You are so nasty." She leaned in and licked his and her juices off his fingers then forced her tongue in his mouth.

"Tonight, we will be the nastiest we have ever been." He firmly warned then bit into her neck as she continued to rock her hips to the beat.

There was no secret about this married couple. They liked to play and if they had an audience the game began even sweeter. Sa'Moo grabbed her by the waist and pulled her onto his lap. He held her in place allowing his dick to grow to her perfect size.

"Mmmm…" she purred as she felt him stiffen between her butt cheeks.

Sa'Moo waved over the dancers they had around him and prepared himself for the show. There they were hidden in the dark corner of VIP surrounded by beautiful woman who danced nicely in front of them stimulating their every pleasure.

Tylinn took his hand and rubbed it over the soft hot flesh as the woman twerked and grinded all over them. She moved her butt slowly against him enjoying the feeling of his hard dick now knocking at the opening of her pussy.

"Raise up," he ordered as he adjusted her wrap.

Tylinn eased up until she could feel his naked flesh against hers. He placed the head at her opening, his knees buckled at how wet she had become. He pushed up inch by inch until he fit perfectly. He pulled Tylinn down onto him with every slow thrust until he felt her quaking.

Tylinn gyrated in a circular motion until she felt his fingertips press into her thigh. She pulled the woman a little closer giving them all the shade they needed so he could bust the pussy the way she needed him too. She allowed her hands to explore their half naked bodies as Sa'Moo pumped faster and faster inside her. He quickened his stroke as her muscles strangled his dick from head to base.

Tylinn wined her waist to the beat of his thrust as she rained her sweet nectar all over his shaft. Up and down she bounced to the beat as the moment seemed to ignite then all.

"Baby," she heard Sa'Moo say then she felt his teeth sink into her back.

Tylinn closed her eyes and let the liquor and passion take her over the top.

Sa'Moo reached up, grabbed her face and turned it to the side, then forced his tongue into her mouth. Tylinn sucked gently as she felt him pulsating between the lips of her pussy.

"I'm fucking you crazy all weekend." He paused to warn her of the trouble she was in.

"Not if I fuck you first." She challenged.

Tylinn sat up then grabbed the hand of a thick Brazilian woman and pulled her to them. She eased her tongue over the woman's lips then slipped it in her mouth. She caressed the woman's breasts, holding her nipples hostage as she enjoyed her taste.

Sa'Moo fought to keep his dick from stiffening as his eyes were caught in visual pleasure. His mouth watered as he watched his wife have perfect lip and tongue play. Tylinn whispered in the woman's ear causing her to blush and smile from ear to ear. She kissed Tylinn one more time then shook her head "no", to whatever Tylinn had asked.

Sa'Moo watched as the woman got back to work dancing and twisting her body with the other ladies paid to make their night perfect. Tylinn reached forward and grabbed the bottle of brown liquor by the neck and poured it into her mouth and then did the same to Sa'Moo.

Sa'Moo swallowed the hot liquid then swayed as the dancers performed right in front of them, then he got back to work. He had another nut he needed to bust, and this was the perfect place to do it. Tylinn arched her back as she felt his inches expanding her walls. The slow deep thrusts sent chills up and down her spin as she anticipated his next move. With ease she grinded her hips into his pelvis matching his push wanting no mercy in return.

Sa'Moo was caught up in a sea of pussy, all he could do was pray that there was no heaven better than this.

****

"This place is amazing." Neena squealed as her eyes danced from one piece of excitement to the next.

"Hell yeah. It's about to be live." Jerome chimed in. He was ready to do things you had to remind yourself to leave right here at the scene of the crime.

"Baby, I don't see any tables." She looked around from one end of the crowded area to the other.

"Let's go to the bar." He said over the thump of the beat then took her hand and led her in the direction of the liquor.

Neena swayed her hips and waved her free arm to the music as he led the way. Jerome leaned in and ordered them a few drinks then turned to watch the fun. The crowd was filling the dancehall and the energy was climbing by the second.

"Here you go." The tiny woman yelled out as she sat the drinks on the bar.

"Damn I thought I was going to have to come behind the bar and make the drinks myself." Jerome said as he took the drinks by the neck and slid then from the stainless-steel top.

"Anything else?" The waitress asked with a smirk at the corner of her lips.

"Nah, we good. Might not get that shit until tomorrow." He spat before bringing the drink to his mouth.

The waitress turned and walked off not dignifying his comment with a response.

"Let's just have a good time." Neena reached over and gripped his arm in an effort to ease his mood.

Jerome didn't reply he just brought his drink back to his mouth and began pouring it down his throat.

Neena removed her hand from his arm and grabbed her drink. she needed to begin numbing her mind. It was going to be a long ass weekend and she was planning to spend the majority of it, drunk. Neena looked around the room and was instantly turned on.

There was wall to wall skin and booth by booth was filled with couples enjoying each other's touch and taste. She was about to ask Jerome to dance when her attention was diverted by the woman and man in VIP who were giving each other the best time ever.

MAKE ME CUM

Erica and Neena, stood at the bar trying to order a drink. They moved closer and closer in the line but were overlooked several times.

"Damn can a bitch get a drink?" Neena said, aloud frustrated with the service.

"Exactly, this is supposed to be paradise. I can't even get drunk." Erica complained, extending her hand to Neena. "I'm Erica, and you."

"Hi, I'm Neena. Nice to meet you. Are you here alone?" She yelled over the music.

"No, unfortunately I brought sand to the beach." Erica rolled her eyes.

"Girrlll…I did the same thing." Neena responded.

"Shieet…I know next time." Erica put her hand up to slap five with Neena.

Neena caught Erica's hand in the air and smacked it twice.

"You ready to order?"

"Yes," Erica said as she leaned in to place her order. "Let me get the drink you have with the most liquor." She giggled as the words left her mouth.

"Make that two." Neena chimed in and winked, holding up two fingers on both of her hands.

"No four." She put up her hands up flashing four fingers, with rocks on at least three of them.

"I got you." The bartender said, then turned to fix their drinks.

Neena and Erica, stood there sharing a few laughs as they waited. When the bartender returned with four tall glasses, filled to the top, with blue liquid dressed with strawberries, and whip cream on top. They each took two glasses by the neck and pulled them close.

"Girl I'm about to get fucked up." Neena said, as she put her plump lips on the straw and sucked.

Erica followed suit taking hers down fast. "Damn," she mumbled as the rush flooded her mind, then coursed through her body. She wasted no time taking another full gulp.

"Bitch we about to have to crawl back." Neena laughed, as they slapped hands, and continued to take the drink down.

"Good, I haven't had a good reason to be on my knees in years," she said as she busted into laugher.

"Sheeiitt…I'ma suck a dick if nothing else. Fuck that, even when I want to have sex I'll suck his dick. I like it." Neena spat as she sucked hard on her straw.

"I'll drink to that," Erica chuckled, also taking another gulp of the frozen delight.

Erica and Neena, looked around the room and almost simultaneously their eyes settled on the VIP section, off to the left. It was Sa'Moo and Tylinn. They had beautiful women all around them, dancing and drinking, while they were engulfed in mouth and hand play. The warm air and loud Caribbean sounds set the mood for the visual pleasure they were receiving, watching the live display.

"That bitch got it made." Erica told Neena.

"Girl, I wouldn't know what to do with myself." Neena responded, as she sipped the last of her first drink, then picked up her second.

The two were halfway through their drink and heavy into the entertainment, when their little show was interrupted.

"What the fuck is taking you so long?" Jerome asked, leaning over Neena's shoulder.

"Baby, this is Erica. Erica, this is my husband Jerome." She quickly diverted his attention to Neena.

"Pleased to meet you." He extended his hand, eyeing her from head to toe.

"The pleasure's all mine." She returned the greeting, as she also looked him over. Her pussy slightly tingled, as he caressed her hand.

Briefly they were caught in a stare down and as their hands began to disconnect, Erica heard her lover's voice.

"Baby girl, I see you met some friends." Mason said, as he approached his wife, and the two strangers standing only inches away.

"You know how I do, baby." She stood up on her tip toes and placed a kiss on his lips. "Baby this is Neena and Jerome. This is my husband, Mason." She made the introduction.

Greetings were passed, and the couples got caught up in conversation, as the women finished the last of their drinks. As the glasses became empty, Mason, turned and ordered a few more drinks and the night began.

"You see that couple?" Erica asked, as the fruity liquor took over her body, then her mind. She grinded her booty on Mason, as the spicy tunes seeped into her soul.

"Hell yeah," Mason responded, as his hands roamed over her ass.

"They been at it for hours." Erica said, as her mind began to wander.

"That's the type of fun a man need," Jerome mumbled, as his eyes settled on Tylinn's perky breasts, sitting high in the tight short dress, that was serving her curves greatness.

"Word." Mason co-signed, pulling Erica into his arms.

The music and liquor, had them all on max, as they watched the freaky display. Erica started to turn her gaze, but was stopped by Tylinn's waving finger, summoning her to their area.

Erica pointed her finger towards her chest as to say, who me?

Tylinn nodded her head up and down, slowly in confirmation.

"Oh, shit baby she just invited us over."

"Word." Mason asked, feeling his dick jump against his zipper.

They looked in Tylinn's direction, to see her pointing at them all to join the party.

Mason looked at Erica, and Jerome, looked at Neena. "Y'all down?" Jerome asked and waited for their response.

"Let's do it." Erica said grabbing Mason by the hand.

Jerome didn't wait for Neena's response. He sat his glass on a nearby table, grabbed her hand, and pulled her through the crowd, right up to the velvet rope.

Security looked back at Sa'Moo who nodded his agreement and they were let through the rope.

"Hi, I'm Tylinn, call me Ty. This is my heart and soul, Sa'Moo. But you can call him 'Moo." She introduced them both in her light Asian accent. "Would you like to join us. We love company." She stated, biting her bottom lip.

"We would love to join you." Mason answered for them all. His eyes and mouth watering at this perfect Asian and black mix packed into a five-foot four-inch body.

"Great, let's have fun," Tylinn said, looking at the waitress who quickly left the area to replenish the drinks.

"What y'all drinking?" Sa'Moo directed his question to Jerome and Mason.

"We ready to wild out, do you." Jerome answered as a thick chocolate woman, in a yellow G-string bikini rubbed her hands up and down his now stiffening dick.

"Cool." Sa'Moo leaned over and whispered in the waitress's ear.

The couples loosened up immediately and began to dance between the sexy women in VIP. When the server returned, with two trays full of shot glasses, filled with white liquor, and as the tray moved the glasses became empty. She left and returned three times before Mason and Jerome threw up their hands.

Erica was in a haze. She looked over at Sa'Moo in his off-white linen shorts and tank top, her mouth watered as Tylinn bent over and twerked her butt against him. She could see the bulge growing down his thigh with every move of Tylinn's waist.

Sa'Moo noticed her intense stare and knew it was time to make his move. He motioned for Tylinn to stand, then mouthed his instructions.

Tylinn sauntered towards Jerome and Mason and Sa'Moo moved to where Neena and Erica were dancing.

"Is this your first time in Brazil?" Sa'Moo asked, as he took Erica and Neena by the hand.

"Yes." They answered in unison, giggling like two high school freshmen.

"Come sit down." He led them to the couch and sat between them. He squeezed the thickness of their hips, as he pulled them closer to his sides.

Tylinn took Mason and Jerome by the hand, lead them to other side, and pushed them down on the soft seats as she then summoned a few dancers to stand in front of them and start a whole new show. The women began to twerk and grind on their laps as the music took control of their movement.

Erica and Neena were filled with nervous jitters, as they watched their husbands being pleasured by the baddest women in the room and enjoying every second.

"No worries. We will all have a good time tonight." Sa'Moo assured, as he slid his hand up each of their thighs.

Erica jumped and closed her legs as his hand got closer to her kitty.

"Relax. I will only give you the pleasure you ask for." He stared firmly into her eyes.

Erica was lost for words and thoughts, as his heat melted her rational mind.

The server returned with two trays filled with tequila shots. Sa'Moo grabbed two shot glasses from the tray. "Here's to a great night. And no regrets in the morning." He held his glass high.

"Salute," the men tuned in and down their drinks.

Erica and Neena, sipped until their glasses were empty and their concision was gone.

When one glass was emptied they were handed another. The waitress made several trips bringing bottle after bottle. She sat two hookahs on the table and they took their turns inhaling the flavored smoke as they downed one shot after the next.

Mason gripped the dancer's hips, as she whined her waist against his now semi-hard dick. He pulled in thick smoke and blew it into the air, as her pussy motions made him feel like he was inside of her instead of outside.

Jerome was sharing the same piece of heaven, as the woman performing for him had now climbed onto his lap and was grinding up and down his body like a well charmed snake.

Tylinn danced and watched as Sa'Moo softened his prey. He rubbed and caressed them as he whispered what she knew was dirty secrets in their ear. She rotated her gaze over to Jerome and Mason who were getting more than fuck ready. She began plotting her night. They had met the life they needed to add to their party of two, and she was planning to get her whole body pleasured.

Tylinn returned to where Sa'Moo sat grabbing a few glasses of hot liquid along the way. She straddled his lap, then placed one glass on Erica's Mouth and one on Neena's. She tilted their heads back putting them right in position and the ladies parted their lips to receive what she was pouring.

Tylinn drizzled the wet heat into their mouths, then allowed it to drip down their chins, onto their breasts.

Erica felt a tingle ease between the lips of her pussy, as Tylinn leaned in and placed her tongue in her mouth.

Tylinn eased her hand into Erica's tank top savoring the softness of her breasts as she rubbed her hands over Erica's stiffened nipples.

"Ssss…" a slight hiss left Erica's mouth. She had never kissed a girl, but tonight she was loving it. There was so many feelings rushing through her body and mind she just closed her eyes and let Tylinn have whatever she wanted.

Tylinn pulled back still rolling Erica's nipples between her fingers. She leaned over and grabbed Neena by the back of her head and kissed her passionately, biting her lips and nibbling on her chin. She rotated between kissing and fondling each woman, while grinding slowly against Sa'Moo.

"Get that shit baby," he mumbled as gripped her waist, guiding her movement.

Sa'Moo placed his lips on hers and kissed her deeply, as Erica and Neena looked on through a glossy stare. Sa'Moo, then slipped his hand between Tylinn's legs and inserted two fingers into her wetness and moved them slowly in and out.

"Oooo…baby," she moaned, as she eased her hand between Neena's legs.

Neena took a deep breath as her body began to heat up. She didn't know what to do, so she sat frozen as Tylinn's fingers moved inside her pussy just right.

"I'm ready for some pussy." Sa'Moo mouthed as he watched Tylinn pleasure all three of them.

"I want my treats too," she moaned as he continued to get her wet.

The club was at capacity, with people from all over the world, wall to wall feeling the same vibe, at the same time. The drinks were flowing along with the warm breeze which had them all on fire.

"Y'all ready to go play," he turned to ask both Neena and Erica.

Caught in the moment they both nodded yes. Tylinn rose to her feet, allowing his hand to slide from her between her thighs. She pulled Erica and Neena to their feet. Erica's eyes were low and she was ready to enjoy whatever the night had to offer.

The moved towards Jerome and Mason who were basically dry humping the entertainment. The both began to stand as the others got close to them.

Tylinn took Jerome by the hand then placed it on her breast.

"Live a little," She whispered then grabbed Erica and kissed her passionately. Tylinn slid her hand between Neena's legs while rubbing Jerome's dick.

Tylinn slide Jerome's hand between her legs, allowing him to feel the wet plumpness between her gap.

"Y'all wanna go play?" Tylinn gave the invitation.

"Hell yeah," Jerome answered without hesitation.

Mason nodded his big head while his other head began to swell.

The invitation was accepted with a nod of the head, and just like that the night was set into motion.

LATE NIGHT LICK LUST, FEAR, & FIRE

Bait and Switch

The limo ride seemed to take forever, as the couples were now engaged in horny touch and play. Mason and Jerome restricted their touch to Neena and Erica, while Sa'Moo took his turn giving each woman a little something special.

When the car came to a stop. The door popped open and the couples were led up the walkway and to the tucked away bungalow.

Mason squeezed Erica's hand then brought it to his chest as they followed close behind, Jerome and Neena. Each of them feeling both excited and insecure. Tylinn and Sa'Moo, unlocked and opened the double wooden doors and stepped inside.

"Wow," Erica said a little above a whisper, her eyes widened, as they entered the living room.

The array of burnt orange and yellow made the room feel warm and inviting. The floor to ceiling windows, allowed them to stare right into the ocean as if they were not separated by walls, and steel.

"This is amazing," Neena joined in, eyeing the open space filed with red and white roses, small and large candles and three very curvy women, dressed in nothing but red thong bikini bottoms.

"Welcome to our home away from home." Tylinn announced as she walked over and turned up the music.

Sa'Moo pulled Tylinn into his chest and wrapped her in his embrace.

"These beautiful women will help you get comfortable and then bring you to the main room. Follow them." He instructed.

They were handed a drink, then led off to separate bedrooms. Once they were behind closed doors the women that were assigned undressed them and led them to the private shower.

Jerome and Neena stood with their arms extended while their hot naked flesh was washed from head to toe. Erica's body formed tiny chill bumps as the soapy sponge slid over her skin. Jerome pulled Neena into his arms and held her tightly under the hot water until they were soap free and ready for the next level of temptation.

The women eased the towel over their skin, massaged them with hot coconut oil then led them to the den of pleasure. They were given one more drink then led naked to the rooms of pleasure.

Erica covered her breasts with one arm and squeezed Mason's hand tightly in her other.

"I'm so nervous," Erica whispered.

"It's all good, baby. Just let go." He reassured her with a wink and slight smile.

They walked behind their escorts naked and slightly trembling. Erica tipped behind Mason thinking, *what have we agreed to?* She clutched his hand in hers as they walked up on Tylinn and Sa'Moo.

Jerome and Neena entered right behind them also dressed in nothing but fear and uncertainty. Jerome became excited when he looked at Tylinn's bare oiled skin. His eyes roamed over her soft round breasts and down her belly to the fatness of her pussy lips.

"Damn," he mumbled as her pussy reminded him of a sweet peach.

Neena looked up at him with glossy eyes, as she prepared herself for what the night would bring.

They were led into an all-white glass, enclosed shower with golden knobs.

"Welcome," Sa'Moo said, as they entered the steamy mist.

Soft music played as each couple took a spot in the warm box. Steam eased between them as Tylinn walked over to Mason and took him by the hand. She then grabbed Jerome by his wrists and brought them to stand next to Sa'Moo.

Once the men were in place, she then led Erica and Neena to where the men stood, positioning them right in front of a husband that was not their own.

Neena stared Jerome in the eyes while Erica rotated her gaze with Sa'Moo. They then explored each other's bodies enjoying eyefuls of soft toned flesh.

"First, we please them. Then they will please, us." Tylinn said as she lowered herself in front of Mason.

"Rule number two. Don't talk just enjoy the moment. Moment by moment." She softly instructed, as she took him into her mouth.

Neena and Erica followed suit and kneeled before their prey.

Erica was in heaven. Right there in her face was over nine inches of thick rock-hard dick. She grabbed him by the sides of his ass cheeks and forced him to back of her throat.

"Mmmm…" she moaned as she began to suck and slurp up and down his length.

Tylinn was only inches away playing with the head of Mason's dick, as she reached over and rubbed Erica's thigh, then over to her now throbbing clit. She circled slowly while tightened her jaws on Mason's dick.

Erica closed her eyes and eased as much of him as she could in and out of her mouth. Her moans increased as Tylinns fingers tickled her slippery pearl just right.

Sa'Moo gripped Erica's ponytail and moved her mouth to his pleasure, her wet tongue wrapped around his shaft as her throat gripped the head with every inward motion.

"Ssss…" he hissed as the suction of her jaws rewarded every inch.

Neena stroked Jerome's rod firmly in her hand allowing only the head to touch her lips. She flicked her tongue back and forth and sucked gently as her right hand stroked to the rhythm of his groans.

The men held their focus on the woman at their waist, occasionally glancing to see the action on the side of them. Erica, Neena and Tylinn worked their mouth action until they were rewarded with sticky passion at the back of their throat.

Tylinn rose first sucking Mason's essence from her fingers.

Sa'Moo rubbed his hand through Erica's hair staring intensely in her eyes. He bit into his bottom lip them gave out the next order of business.

"A wife for a wife." Sa'Moo took Erica and Neena by the hand and led them out of the shower. "Enjoy." He said before disappearing with both woman.

Jerome turned to Tylinn and began sucking her lips as he caressed both of her breasts in his hands. He rolled her hardened nipples between his fingers then placed them in his mouth.

Mason stroked his dick while watching Jerome fill his hands and mouth with Tylinn's sweet treasures. Unable to control anymore of his urges, he lowered himself to her waist, placed her leg over his shoulder and went to work on the pink that was glistening between two soft thighs. He devoured her burying his fast and tongue, moving along with the gyration of her hips.

"Yes…yesss…" she moaned as she felt his tongue flip faster on her clit. Her body was ready to reward him, so she did just what she needed to do. Let go.

Mason lapped at her juices as they dripped into his mouth and down his chin.

Jerome sucked and nibbled on her erect nipples intensifying every spasm. When Tylinn caught her breath, she moved her leg from his shoulder, pulled him to her, eased her tongue into his mouth, then savored his thick lips.

Tylinn pulled back, took them by the hand, then led them out of the shower, into the bedroom just across the hall.

Jerome stood looking over Tylinn's perfect body and his mouth watered at the fantasy, playing loudly in his mind.

They were welcomed to the room by slow soft music and flames dancing nicely on wax. They stepped inside closed the door behind them and moved Tylinn to the middle of the room where they could now enjoy all of her.

Tylinn stood just inches away from two hungry wolves and she was ready to be consumed. She eased her hands over her breasts and belly, then positioned them between her legs.

Mason's dick stood straight out, as he watched her separate her pussy lips and play between them. The glistening juices against her puffy pink lips made him want to plunge deep. He wanted to be inside of her and he wanted to make sure he was the one inside her first.

Mason moved towards her and placed his hands on hers. He pushed his fingers deep inside her and took each breath as she exhaled. As he moved them faster and faster inside her, Tylinn's pussy rotated against him moving in sync with his every movement. He bit into her neck and nibbled her collar bone as she gripped his arms and nuzzled her forehead on his chest.

Jerome stroked himself back to life, as he watched her body began to jerk against Mason. Her moans and cries for more had him on the edge ready to bust all over her.

"Get on the bed." Mason instructed as he turned her body and followed close behind.

Tylinn positioned her now drunken frame in the middle of the king-sized bed and got on all fours, with a perfect full arch in her back. She bit into her bottom lip, as Mason got behind her, and Jerome got in front.

Mason wasted no time pushing his stiff inches deep inside her tender wet hole. He gripped her hips and pulled her into him, changing angles with every stroke.

"Mmm…" Mason mumbled, as he pounded her from the back.

Tylinn gripped Jerome's dick and put it into her mouth. She sucked forcefully, as she enjoyed the power strokes from the back.

"Ahhh…yessss…make me cum." She moaned between slurping and gagging on the hardness she had against her jaw.

Mason was in heaven. Her pussy was tight and wet. Her warm walls caressed his inches as he deep dicked her from behind. Mason watched his sweat drip onto her ass cheeks as they giggled against him.

Tylinn threw her ass against his thighs causing a friction on his dick, that made his knees weak. His stomach knotted up, as his balls were now ready to empty.

Jerome was also barely holding on, as her tongue and throat had his dick feeling right at home. He gripped the back of her head, pushed her all the way down on him, and pulled her quickly back and forth.

Tylinn gripped his ass and made sure he could not escape, as she gave him what he was asking for. She gagged and swallowed him, tightening her jaws, with every movement until she felt him attempt to pull back.

"Oh ssshit…" he moaned trying to balance himself with his other hand.

Tylinn showed no mercy, she worked her head and neck, until his seed was sliding down the back of her throat. She kept working, causing him to fall slightly back.

Mason turned on by her mouth work, fucked faster, and faster to bring on his satisfaction. He pumped and pumped, until he felt the tingle release from his gut. Tylinn allowed Jerome to ease out of her mouth, braced her arms, and pushed back into Mason as he pumped into her.

Mason pushed her forward, climbed onto her back, and fucked fast and hard until his nuts were empty. He fell on top of her breathing heavy as she jerked beneath him.

"Mmmm...that was good. I want more." She whispered as she lifted her head and began kissing the tip of Jerome's dick.

Tylinn rose up from the bed causing Mason to get up as well. She turned her back to Jerome and looked Mason in his eyes with a hunger to taste her juices on his dick. She lowered herself to his waist and began to revive his solider.

Jerome rubbed the head of his dick on her wet opening and with every touch he got thicker. He pushed and rubbed until he was inside her warm place, then went to work.

Mason grabbed a pillow, propped it under his head, and laid back to enjoy the show. He stared in Tylinn's eyes as Jerome slowly fucked her pussy from the back.

Tylinn matched his stock by playfully sucking and licking the head of Mason's dick, while enjoying Jerome's thin hook playing with her spot.

Jerome reached around and tickled her clit as he stroked to the rhythm of her every moan and whimper. It was going to be a long night. He was planning to have her pussy, in every position he could think of, making sure not to miss an invitation to any hole she needed to have pleased.

****

Sa'Moo laid Neena on the bed and placed Erica right next to her. He took his time giving each woman's body the attention it needed. He rotated licking and sucking gently on their erect nipples causing their pussy juices to flow freely down their lower lips. They moaned and squirmed as he inserted two fingers deep inside them and fucked them slowly.

"Keep your legs open." He ordered as Erica clamped her thighs on his arm. He sank his teeth into the fatness of Erica's breast, while pleasuring her tight hole until her body responded with loud cries of passion.

As Erica's legs quivered Sa'Moo eased his wet fingers out of her hot spot, then positioned himself over Neena's necked hot body and spread her legs wide. He traced the tip of his tongue along her stomach circling slowly before taking it into his mouth. He sucked her clit until it was swollen and asking for more. Sa'Moo played between her thighs with his tongue until her body squirmed and shivered.

"Moo…" she moaned as she gripped the sides of his face.

Erica rubbed one of her hands up and down her wet pussy lips and with the other she squeezed her nipples between her fingers anxiously awaiting her turn.

Sa'Moo sensing the impatience pulled her over to join them. He flipped her over placing her between Neena's legs and almost on cue Erica began to lap at Neena's tender clit.

Erica opened Neena's lips and sucked and licked as she reached up and rolled her nipples between her fingers.

Sa'Moo kissed and nibbled up and down Erica's spine as he watched her taste and moan. He spread Erica's butt cheeks apart and slid his tongue down the crack of her soft round butt, until his mouth fit perfectly over her pussy lips. He stuck his tongue in and out of her lapping at all her juices.

Sa'Moo kissed along her juicy lips, stopping only to replace his tongue with two, then three fingers. Erica rocked back into his push feeling electrical surges travel from her head to the tip of her toes.

Sa'Moo was ready to open her up. He rose up on his knees and lifted her to fit onto his dick, then slowly eased his way in.

"Ahhh..." Erica moaned as she threw one hand back to slow his push.

"Move your hand and eat." Sa'Moo ordered as he pushed her hand away and continued to force his thick inches into her very tight space.

"Damn," Sa'Moo mumbled as he forced himself deeper. It felt like she hadn't been fucked in years.

"Oh...my...God..." Erica stuttered as she felt his dick tear into her.

Erica's eyes filled with lustful tears, as her pussy tried to accommodate Sa'Moo's inches. She traced her soft tongue along Neena's inner thigh. She lapped at her swollen pearl until she heard passion escape her mouth.

Sa'Moo pulled her into him with ease, as he opened her up. He admired her pecan skin and plump butt as it slapped against his thighs. The arch in her back and thin waist made him want to pound her for hours. Sa'Moo gave her kitty what it was calling for. With every thrust and every push, she moaned louder for more, he was treating her pussy like it was his, and her lips were saying *yes*, with every thick stroke.

His mouth watered as her pussy strangled his dick making the ride even sweeter.

Neena was turned on even more when she looked up at Sa'Moo's chiseled chest tensing up played against her walls. He pumped into Erica trembling womb enjoying the pain and pleasure on her face. Erica's soft, round breasts jiggled with his every motion, causing Neena to want them in her mouth. She reached down and placed her hands on the top of Erica's head trying to ease her grip as she showed her clit no mercy. Erica closed her eyes and enjoyed the taste of her silky wetness as she soaked the sheets.

"Ssss… I'm cumming." Neena said gripping Erica's hair.

Sa'Moo fucked faster as he watched Neena's juices squirt onto Erica's face.

"Mmmm…" Erica moaned as she rubbed her face in the wetness.

"Shit," he groaned as Erica's pussy tightened.

Erica pushed back into him until she shook and screamed. Sa'Moo felt as if he was breaking something as he rammed until she was unable to move or run. Erica dropped her head and bit into Neena's inner thigh as she creamed all over his throbbing shaft.

"Oh my God," she said with a heavy breath.

Sa'Moo was in his glory, he quickly switched positions. He laid on his back and placed Erica on his dick and Neena on his face. He sank his fingertips into the soft flesh of her ass pulling her whole pussy into his mouth. Sa'Moo flipped his tongue slowly back and forth tickling her pearl until soft moans left her mouth. She rolled her pelvis against his face riding to the rhythm of his tongue. The louder she moaned the harder he sucked on her clit.

Erica slid up and down on his dick chanting his name as she rode.

"Moo… Mooooo…" she called out as she bounced to the sound of her slippery pussy.

Each time he made an upward thrust she bit into her bottom lip and braced herself for every entry.

Neena placed her hands on the wall as Sa'Moo sucked the very life from her body.

"Oh, my God. Mooo…Wait…" She screamed as her pussy jerked, then sprayed its nectar all over his lips.

Neena rotated her hips on his mouth as he licked at her luscious lips.

Erica hopped up and down until her juices rained down on his thickness. She rose to her feet, letting his stiff dick slide from her throbbing insides. She positioned herself at his waist and sucked on the precious jewels.

Neena wiggled away from his grip and joined Erica to taste the passion that lingered from her sweet spot. They licked and savored Erica's essence from his stiffness all while looking up at the king as they worshiped his throne.

Sa'Moo laid back and watched his two beauties pleasure him, while planning the next position to have them in. He and Tylinn had played this game with dozens of couples, but not until today had he been in a position, to have exactly what he wanted.

This was the first time he questioned if their rules worked, or would he have to bite the forbidden fruit one more time.

The Morning After

By the time the sun broke the horizon, each couple was comfortably laying in their designated rooms in a sea of soft feather pillows and red silky sheets.

Jerome looked over at Neena's limp body and his mind wondered about what happened with her and Sa'Moo while he was only feet away fucking his wife. His eyes settled on each of the red and blue marks on her back. Another man had sprayed on his territory and left the marks to prove it.

There she lay only inches from his side sleeping as if she had the best dick ever and the reality of the night hit him, as much as he had enjoyed himself he would never want to have his wife in another man's hands.

Jerome eased up behind Neena and just wrapped his arms around her and held her tightly. He inhaled enjoying the perfume on her skin. Neena placed her hand on top of his and took a deep breath as she too was relieved to be in the arms of the man she loved.

****

Erica eased off the cool sheets, tipped into the bathroom and closed the door behind her. She clicked the locks then stood in front of the mirror looking her body over. She giggled as she remembered everything Sa'Moo did to her body and her mind. For the first time in years she was completely satisfied. She twirled from side to side and moved her hands along her naked frame.

When she turned to see his hand prints on her ass. She closed her eyes and reminisced. Her pussy lips got wetter and wetter as her mind focused in on that pretty, long dick that dangled perfectly between his legs.

"The best vacation ever." She said aloud as she reached over and grabbed a towel and wash cloth.

Erica turned on the shower, got the temperature just right and stepped inside. She lathered her skin and inhaled the steam as she again dozed off into the heat of last night. She had been craving the type of gut wrenching orgasms that Sa'Moo had given her and now she was going to find it hard to just walk away from those feelings.

****

Almost simultaneously the bedroom doors opened. Erica and Mason locked eyes with Neena and Jerome for the first time since they stepped out of the Limo.

"Good morning," Mason took the lead needing to break the awkwardness.

"Good Morning," Neena and Jerome responded at the same time.

"Y'all look how we feel." Mason joked as they took turns moving into the hallway.

42

"Last night was fucking epic," Jerome responded.

"A movie." Erica mumbled under her breath as she switched her ass with every stride.

****

The week was long and eventful. Erica and Mason had hiked and swam, they ziplined, shopped, ate great food, and hopped around from one parade to the next.

Erica let her arms drop to the side as the powerful hands moved over her body. A massage was the perfect ending to a great week. She had tasted the forbidden fruit and now her sweet tooth had a craving. She had no regrets.

Erica relaxed into the moment and tried to release the last of her stress before leaving paradise. She was enjoying the slippery touch of magic hands when she felt one of those hands slide down her butt and between her legs.

"What the fuck." She quickly lifted her head.

Sa'Moo put his finger up to his mouth then slid Erica to the edge of the table.

"Wait." She whispered as he eased up behind her.

"I need you," Sa'Moo also whispered as he spread her cheeks and slid in not waiting for a response.

Sa'Moo began stroking to the sounds of her muffled moans. He gripped her ass just right until he had her in a full buck.

"Ahhh…yesss…" she mumbled gripping the edge of the table.

Erica closed her eyes and thought about the last time he was from the back, she had a mouth full of Erica's sweet pussy. She reveled in the memories as her pussy heated up, drenching him with every stroke. She pushed back into him as he pounded away.

"Damn," Sa'Moo mumbled as he pushed faster.

"Yesss… I'm about to cum." She began gyrating and twerking against him as he hit her spot.

"Gimme this pussy," he ordered showing no mercy.

Sa'Moo pulled her from the table, bent her all the way over, and went into fuck mode.

Erica braced her hands on the floor and took all his inches with pride. Her moans got louder as her legs began to shake beneath her.

Sa'Moo fucked her right through her contractions intensifying the moment as he reached his release. He pulled her back and forth until he felt his balls drain. He pushed in deep and let go holding her firmly in place.

Erica remained bent over trying to catch her breath as she felt him slip from between the lips of her now swollen pussy.

Sa'Moo pulled her up into his chest. He kissed her softly on her lips then nibbled her neck. The heat between them was mind blowing. Erica pulled back, grabbed her robe from the chair and slipped it on.

"Shhh...our little secret." Sa'Moo whispered as he pulled up his trunks and headed to the door.

Erica pulled the robe up on her shoulders and closed it tightly. She could feel his hot seed easing out of her and down her inner thigh. Guilt filled her chest as the weight of the promise she just broke held her body in place like an anchor. She focused her sight on a speck of sand on the carpet and a drunken smile caressed the corners of her mouth.

What was done was done. There was no turning back. And guilt would only mess up the pleasure he had just given her whole body.

****

Sunday morning had come all too fast. She moved in what seemed like slow motion as she placed the neatly folded items into their suit cases. She took one more look around then headed into the bathroom.

Erica played over and over in her mind the night that had changed her life. She became sick to her stomach when she thought of going home with Mason and receiving his touch. Erica could not stand the idea of having to make love to him again after she had just gotten all her fantasies fulfilled in the matter of hours.

How could she go back to life as usual when she would be just going through the motions?

Erica looked for Sa'Moo everywhere they went. But she had no luck. She sighed as she placed the last of their things in the suit cases then zipped them closed. She walked around the room making sure they had all of their things.

Erica sat on the bed, put her face in the palm of her hands and tried to change the funky mood she was in. She was just about to recover when Mason walked in.

"So, I checked us out." He said entering the room. He closed the door then headed to where she sat.

"Did you make sure to have them take the parking out of the business card?" she asked as she looked up from her hands.

"Yes. You okay?" He asked with a wrinkled brow.

"I'm fine." She mustered up a smile. "Just not looking forward to all the work on my desk." She walked over, grabbed her purse and copy of the room key card.

"Well don't worry baby. We had an epic time to remember as you get back to the grind." He said as he collected the suit cases and headed to the door.

"I'll meet you at the elevator." He walked over and kissed her forehead.

Mason then opened the door wide and pilled the bags onto the luggage cart. Erica took one last look into the mirror adjusting her yellow backless sundress. She put on her shades and walked out behind him.

****

46

Neena stood looking over the array of exotic fruit and muffins on the breakfast buffet. She grabbed a few grapes, star fruit and orange slices. She placed a boiled egg and bacon strips on the side then glanced the area for any other options.

Neena walked over to the juice bar and topped off her meal with a blueberry bagel which she toasted and smeared with cream cheese. She then finished her array of food with a tall glass of orange juice.

Neena walked over to an empty table, placed her plates down and took a seat. She wasted no time diving in. She was caught up in nibbling away when she looked up and saw Erica and Mason checking out.

"Baby I'll be right back." Erica quickly said as Mason handed the receptionist at the front desk his credit card.

"You good?"

"Yes, I'm good. I'm going to grab some coffee." She lied then headed in Neena's direction.

Mason kept his focus on the receptionist as Erica sashayed away.

"Hey mama." She said to Neena as she approached the table.

"Hey girl." Neena responded covering her mouth to finish. "Are y'all checking out." She stood to greet Erica.

"Yes, I hate to go…buu…tt…back to real life."

"You look amazing." Neena looked Erica from head to toe.

"Thanks mama. Just a little something, something."

"Please travel safely. Thank you so much for an amazing time." Neena reached her arms out.

"No, Thank you. Y'all enjoy the rest of the summer." Erica said as she walked into Neena's embrace.

They hugged then backed up exchanging goodbyes' then parted ways. By the time Erica turned around the smile she had plastered had slid off her face.

"You okay, baby?" Mason asked taking her hand.

"Yes." She tried to quickly recover.

"Was that Neena?' he asked trying to look around Erica as she walked swiftly to the hotel exit.

"Yes. I was just saying goodbye." She tried to hide her disappointment. Truth be told Sa'Moo was the only face she wanted to see.

Mason sensed her mood change but didn't address it. He had just had the best week of his life. He felt like he was floating on air, and her funky ass attitude was not gonna knock him out of the clouds. He opened the cab door tucked her inside and floated to the other. He had his one wish. His one night. Nothing could take that away from him.

The Red Eye

Erica was placing her bags in the overhead bin when she looked pass the line of passengers and saw Sa'Moo and Tylinn sitting in first class. She closed the door and slid into her seat occasionally peeking over the seat in front of her to see if she could catch either of them looking back.

"You gonna order something to drink?" Jerome asked as he took her hand and kissed it gently.

"Yes, I need something after the weekend we just had." She looked over at him.

"That was one time. We needed it. Maybe this will help us get back on track." He confessed.

"You are right. Thank you for such a great time." She returned then kissed his lips gently. "I love you."

"I love you too."

The flight attendant returned took their order once the drinks were good and in their system. Jerome turned to the window and dosed off.

Erica unbuckled her seat belt and headed to the back of the plane to use the bathroom. There was a line already formed so she just joined the end and proceeded to wait her turn.

"Can I stand here?" Sa'Moo asked placing himself right behind her.

Erica was paralyzed with fear afraid to turn in his direction, so she answered without looking his way. "Yes, I think it's free to stand," she tried to lighten the mood.

"Cool. But I think I will take a seat right here." Sa'Moo said as he slid into the empty seat next to where she was standing.

Erica looked down at him then back forward afraid that she might act on the five hundred feelings running through her body.

Oh God please hurry. Erica stood there silently praying the line would move but to her surprise it hadn't moved an inch.

Sa'Moo sensed her hesitance and wanted to relax the moment so instead of leaving her there to deal with the sensations arising he knew what she needed to ease her pain. Sa'Moo reached over and put his hand in the opening of her wrap skirt. He wasted no time as he had none to waste. He went right for her clit and circled quickly.

Erica gripped the headrest of the seat in front of her as she tried to hold her balance with his fingers dancing between her legs causing a flood between her now swollen lips.

Sa'Moo rotated between her clit and pushed his fingers deep inside her.

Soft moans left her lips as she tried to keep her eyes open and focused in front of her.

Sa'Moo sped up his tease as he felt her walls tighten on his fingers. He had the spot and wasn't going to let it go. The line moved slightly but she could not move with it. She was on the verge and he wasn't going to stop until he had what he wanted. Faster and faster he tickled her spot until she gushed down sweet wetness all over his fingers.

Erica struggled to catch her breath as her eyes opened. Embarrassment filled her gut as she met gazes with the flight attendant who had just poured her and Mason's drinks.

Sa'Moo rubbed his fingers between the lips of her pussy a few more seconds causing her body to jerk with every touch. He slid his hand from between her thighs and brought his fingers to his mouth. He licked her nectar then stood tall in front of her.

"Our little secret." He whispered. "I'm going to miss the way you taste." He said as he took his place back in line behind her. Sa'Moo allowed his dick to rock up between her ass cheeks causing her to lose her breath.

"I want to fuck you." He confessed grabbing her waist, pulling her back into him. "Can't you feel me? Can't' you feel how good I feel when my dick hits them tight walls?" He teased.

Erica moved up in line while trying to keep her legs closed to avoid the warm liquid from sliding down her leg as his dick rested perfectly against her ass. She wanted to push him in that empty seat and sit on his face, then lay with her legs high in the air and let him fuck her into a coma.

"Thank you," he mumbled in her ear as he took the opportunity to have one last feel of her wet kitty.

Sa'Moo stared hungrily at her ignoring the wondering eyes of the woman in uniform only feet away from them. He pulled Erica into him as he played between her legs. "Cum for me one more time." He circled his finger on her clit. "Cum for me, baby. Cummm…" he ordered showing her clit no mercy.

Erica put her head on his chest, as she tried to control the orgasm that was now taking over her body. She jerked against his strong body.

Sa'Moo held her close to him while she caught her breath. "You good?" He asked as her head lifted from his chest.

"Next," she heard the flight attendant yell just in time. Things were getting hot and she was losing the battle with her rational thoughts.

"You got some good pussy. Enjoy your flight." He released her from his grip. Sa'Moo walked back to his seat with his mission accomplished.

Erica hurried into the bathroom and locked the door behind her. She peed then washed everything she could as fast as she could. She dried off applied some lip gloss and perfume and prepared herself for what was on the other side of the door. She prayed for him to be gone by the time she walked out, and to her benefit he was nowhere in sight when she emerged. Erica took a deep breath and walked quickly back to her seat.

"You okay?" Mason asked, awakened from his little nap as she fidgeted with the seatbelt.

"Yes. I think I got a little flight sick is all."

"Try to rest baby." He rubbed her arm and closed his eyes once again.

Erica had a sigh of relief as she peeked over the seat this time not seeing Sa'Moo at all. He had changed seats with Tylinn and now she could only see her. She took a few deep breaths then closed her eyes and tried to erase everything about this weekend. The strangers they had met were dangerous.

The trip was to restore their marriage not break things into pieces. She tucked all desire and promised herself, that what happened was over and there was no way they could ever let it happen again.

LATE NIGHT LICK LUST, FEAR, & FIRE

Back to Life

Erica sat at her desk staring at the clock as the seconds seemed to tick by like a slow coffee drip. It felt like the day would never end.

"Shit if I can just make it to lunch." She whispered to herself as she shuffled a few papers around on her desk.

She reached down into her purse for her cell phone charger and plugged herself in. She flipped to her gallery and thumbed through the vacation photos. She stopped on a selfie they took in the club right before they left, and her mind drifted to that night and the pleasure she received.

Erica squeezed her thighs as she thought about how good Sa'Moo felt inside her and how badly she wanted him back between her legs. Her clit began to tick against the lace of her thong and wetness filled her lips as the memories of his tongue lapping at her throbbing lips sent chills from her head down to her spin.

Erica could feel his strong hands and soft lips all over her body. She closed her eyes and imagined riding his dick with her back against his chest as his warm breath caressed her earlobe.

"Hey E. What time we leaving for lunch? I need to hear every detail of that trip because you came in here this morning like a brand-new bitch. I want some of that." Sherry leaned against her desk with her arms folded.

Erica snapped out of her day dream with a little bit of anger as she hated to leave her new happy place.

"Hey Sherry. I'll be ready at noon," she answered gazing at the hands on the clock.

"Cool." She said with a raised brow. "Where were you? I feel like I just snatched you out the sky." She giggled at how Erica looked when she entered her office.

A smile crept across her lips. "Girlll… I will fill you in at lunch."

"Oh, shit let me act like I work here for the next hour. I sooo… need this in my life." She turned and hurried back to her station.

Erica pushed her thoughts to the back of mind for now and focused on making the pile on her desk smaller. She snatched up a few files and began entering information into her laptop. Once she got into her work the hour had passed and she was ready to sit and share with her friend the amazing adventure she had.

Erica closed the screen, grabbed her purse from under the desk and headed to the door. She reached in her bag and rolled on some flavored gloss as she headed towards the elevator.

"What's up?" She asked tapping her watch. "I'ma be meeting you down stairs.

"I'm coming," Shery whispered trying to keep the phone from her mouth.

Erica waved at Sherry on her way to the elevator and mouthed, "See you downstairs."

Sherry rolled her eyes, she had been trying to get the investor off the phone for the last twenty minutes. "Yes sir, we can insure that much." She said then hit the mute button.

"Dont leave me." She mouthed. "I want to smack him. Don't eat without me." She said aloud as she watched Erica get on the elevator. "Yes sir. I am here to help." She unmuted and joined in as if she never left.

Erica exited the elevator walking tall and feeling better than she had ever felt.

****

"Babbbyyy… I'm home," Erica announced as she tossed her purse on the table and headed to Mason's home office.

"Hey baby," he said looking up from the set of contracts on his desk. He rose to his feet as she headed in his direction.

Erica walked over to him with a smile and wrapped her arms around his neck.

"I missed you today baby." She confessed kissing him gently in the lips.

"I missed you too." He returned as he kissed her lips and cheeks.

"What do you want for dinner?" Erica asked as he released her from his grip.

"My taste has changed these days," he said looking at her as if she was on the menu.

"Oh really?" She responded as she eased up her skirt until it was up over her butt.

Mason sat back in his chair then gripped her thighs. He moved his hands to her waistline then slid her up onto his desk.

Erica spread her legs wide as he planted kisses on her inner thighs. He inhaled her scent as he began to flip his tongue against her clit.

"Mmmm..." she moaned as Jerome sucked gentle then hard.

Mason savored every lick as she rotated her hips against his face. A weekend he thought would be just a getaway had been the saving grace to their relationship. However, Erica was feeling Mason but picturing Sa'Moo. He had touched her in a way that she feared Mason would never be able to follow.

Confessions

Neena moved around her kitchen getting things straight for her best friend. They had been back from the trip for a month now and with all her work. She hadn't spent any time with her family or friends. However, tonight, her best friend was in town on business and it was about to be a girl's night that she desperately needed.

Neena placed a few small glass dishes on the table with an array of cheese, crackers, and dip, then two dishes with lemon pepper steamed shrimp and Cajun shrimp, topped off with a variety platter of Sushi. She placed two bottles of red wine in the silver chillers and sat two wine flutes next to it. Neena lite a few candles, then popped in Ledisi. She turned up the volume, then headed to the kitchen to check on the main course.

Brielle pulled up to the huge, ranch style home, and parked right in the front. She rushed out of her vehicle, grabbed her bag from the back seat, and ran up to the door.

'Ding…Dong!' She pressed he bell, then fumbled with her bags and purse as she waited.

"Diivvaaaa…" Neena screamed snatching the door open.

"Diva! Diva! Diivvaaaa…" Brielle said, as she jumped on Neena almost knocking her to the floor.

"I missed you so much, my Bre-Bre," she swooned as she hugged her friend tight.

"Well I am here bitch," she sang out again as they loosened their grip.

"It's about to go down," Brielle shouted, tossing her bag against the wall, then she kicked off her shoes, and was ready for the night.

"Girl, I am ready, I need this night." Neena said leading the way into the living-room.

"Mmmm…it smells good in here." Brielle said looking around, admiring the black and white color scheme they had throughout the house.

"Well, I have a few things prepared and planned." Neena said, as she opened the oven to check on Brielle's favorite, meat loaf.

"Girl, this new look is amazing." Brielle said, as she sat on the couch in front of the array of Hors d'oeuvres.

"Girl, it took forever, but we finally got it done." Neena replied, as she opened a bottle of wine.

"Well it paid off. How is Jerome feeling about all the money you spent?" She asked reaching for a wine flute.

"As if I care. Shit my money good at the store too." She chuckled. "Nah, but to be honest. He has been really going out of his way to make sure I am happy." She paused to fill Brielle's glass.

"Well that's the important part. If you are happy, I am happy." She lifted her glass.

Neena filled her own glass to the top, then met Brielle mid-air.

"Here's to over twenty-five years of friendship," Neena toasted.

"Cheers. But, bitch I'm only twenty-one. So, I don't know who the hell you've been friends with those other five or six years." She busted out laughing. "Out here having ghost ass relationships. Get help bitch."

Neena dribbled wine down her chin as she tried to contain her laughter. "I can't stand you." She laughed as she tried to catch the liquid dripped off her chin.

"Whatever." Brielle said taking a sip. "And where is the meat and potatoes. This ain't Martha's Vineyard." She reached for a piece of cheese.

"You know what. I am not doing this with you today." Neena continued to laugh.

The two ladies sat and exchanged laughter and caught each other up on work and personal life. Neena carved up the meatloaf and served it with garlic ranch mashed potatoes, sweet glazed carrots, roasted asparagus, and homemade cheddar biscuits.

"Damn, bitch if I was into women Jerome would be living in the pool house taking care of us both." She joked as she bit into the food mouthful after mouthful.

"You need prayer," Neena laughed enjoying her meal and best friend.

When the ladies finished their meal, they cleared the table. Neena showed Brielle to the guest room, then headed to her room to shower and change. The ladies met back in the kitchen, grabbed the wine and a few snacks, and headed to the basement to watch their favorite movies and shows.

"Girl, that meal was amazing. And these pajamas are official," she danced around pumping and gyrating.

"You are a fool." Neena said, as she grabbed the remote controls and tuned up the television to movie number one.

They got settled on the high-backed, long suede couches, then pulled the cashmere blankets over their legs.

Before the movie got started good Brielle began running off her questions.

"Before we get to the next level of this amazing night." She brought her glass to her lips. "What happen in Brazil, that you were going to so-called tell me about when you see me." She put the ball in Neena's court.

Neena took a deep breath smiled and then searched for the words to reveal her hidden pleasure.

"Do not judge me." Neena said preparing her friend for what she was about to say.

"You know, I will not judge you," Brielle said with a little concern.

"Well. I had way more to eat then just seafood." She said then took a huge gulp of the wine.

"Huh?" Brielle asked with her brow raised.

"Okay." Neena took another deep breath. "We met a couple. We danced, drank and played, and then ended up in their beds." She paused and looked at her friend.

Brielle, was silent as she processed this new information.

"So, hold on. Are you telling me y'all was out there swinging?" She sat up as the conversation was getting juicy.

"Something like that." She stared off as the memories flooded her mind. "Jerome and this guy named Mason the

62

husband of the other woman went into a room with Tylinn."

"Who the hell is, Tylinn?" She asked now confused.

"The wife of the man who snatched my entire damn soul." She confessed.

"Damn." Brielle mumbled as she sat waiting for more.

"His name is Sa'Moo, he's over six-feet tall, cocoa brown-skinned. light brown eyes and a ten-inch dick with the stroke game of a God." She stated shaking her head as the thought of the orgasms had her in waves of multiples.

"Well shit. Then what happened?"

"We were in an amazing room and that man pleased me and Erica as if we were his own personal sex goddess."

"Word," she slurred, sitting on the edge of her seat.

"I have never been touched the way that man touched me, and I have never came, as hard as I did when he was inside me." She again stared off at the wall.

Brielle looked at her friend relive the moments as if they were on the wide screen inched away from them. She saw a happiness in her eyes, but she also saw a craving.

"So, let me get this shit straight. You and another woman got dicked down by that woman's husband. While only a short distance away your husband was train fucking another woman."

Neena thought about what she said and had to chuckle. "Not exactly, and who still says train?" She looked over at her friend.

"So, let me get this straight, also while I'm here. Your tight attitude ass, jealous husband was down to let you fuck another nigga?" She brought the glass to her lips and sipped slow.

"Girrllll...all I know was the drinks were going around. They were touching us and saying some unreal shit. And before you know it I was getting fucked from the back and eating pussy at the same damn time.

"Bitch I'm sleep," Brielle put her head back and closed her eyes.

"You so stupid," she burst out laughing. "Stop be serious, I'm trying to confess my sins." She pulled on Brielle's arm.

"Hold on bitch I need thirty more seconds." She continued to lay to the side.

Neena could do nothing but laugh at her friend.

"Okay, I'm up. So, you were saying something about eating pussy." She joked. "So, now what?" She asked and waited on bated breath for her response.

"I don't know. Some days I crave him. Other days I feel ashamed." She again paused. "But I will say, I am happy I had the experience."

"Well I hear that. Live your best life." She raised her glass. "Here's to living your best life and eating and sucking foreign dick and pussy along the way." She clinked glasses with Neena.

"That's why I love you." She smiled and drank to the toast.

Neena went back and forth with Brielle explaining how everything went down. They finished two more bottles of wine and half watched two movies. By the time they finished going over Neena's sexcapade they were drunk and emotionally wiped out.

"Bitch I can't move." Brielle said pulling the blanket to her chest.

"Me either." Neena responded barley able to keep her eyes open. "I guess we are sleeping right here."

"Yes, we are. And if you get the urge for something to eat in the middle of the night, get some of that shrimp and cheese. Don't touch my cookies."

"I hate you." Neena giggled.

They chuckled a little more before dozing off. Morning came and Neena adjusted her eyes trying to find her slippers in the dimly lit room. She looked over and Brielle and smiled at the thought of having a real rider on her side. She pulled adjusted her blanket then left the room.

Neena headed upstairs, undressed, and jumped right in the shower. She thought about what Brielle said, *what's next*. She didn't have an answer but now that the question was on the table she needed to search for the answer.

LATE NIGHT LICK LUST, FEAR, & FIRE

Hole in One

"Yo, what's good dude?" Jay yelled out to Mason and his brother Rass as he walked in the private pool room.

"I can't call it." Mason responded bumping fists with his best friend.

"Who buying?" Jay asked looking around at the servers in the tight black booty shorts and bikini tops.

"Nah man. Your money ain't no good here. We got it." He leaned over the pool table and sank the yellow stripped ball.

"Nah brah, the last time you were talking shit." Jay said bursting into laughter.

Jay took two one-hundred dollar bills out of his pocket and slapped them on the hard wood lacing the pool table.

"Fuck that, grab that money. I can eat with that," Rass joined in reaching for the crispy bills.

"Nah playa, he said my money no good here," he played around in an Asian accent as he snatched up the bills and tucked them back in his pocket.

Rass playfully jabbed at Jay, they slapped hands a few times then bumped shoulders.

Laughter and slick statements went back and forth as the night got started. Mason had booked a private night of fun. The sexy servers moved through the small intimate party of twelve. They filled their shot glasses with high priced Cognac and lit the ends of their Cuban cigars.

The women then began to entertain. They danced and performed as they stripped out of their shorts and tops, down to only their G-strings. He wanted to introduce his brothers to the pleasure he had in Brazil.

The DJ turned up the music and the booties bounced to the beat. It was private pool night with twelve of Mason's closest friends. He had more than pool planned for the night. He had planned to treat his boys to some new holes, that they could put one in. There was chocolate, vanilla and caramel all around the room and they were about to have a taste, one flavor at a time.

Mason looked around to see that his boys were getting very comfortable. They were being fed drinks and dreams and they were soaking them all up.

Rass was in one corner with his long six foot four-inch frame stretched out while a thick Spanish bad body gave him the grind action of life.

Sweat formed on the top of his chocolate bald head as she slowly whined her waist awakening the beast beneath his zipper. His hands were firmly placed on her tiny waist as she popped that pussy against his now stiffened dick.

"This what a man needs after a long day," Rass yelled out as he allowed himself to grow bigger between her butt cheeks.

"Let me give it to you then papi," she purred in her Spanish accent flipping her hair as she gave him that over the shoulder fuck me look.

Mason smiled as he moved through the room. All his male guests were seated and getting a treat. He walked over to the lights and dimmed them low.

The room went black except for a few neon lights and decorations throughout the room.

Mason gripped the hand of the woman designated to give him his late night special.

Once he was comfortable in his seat, he gave the dancers the signal and the thongs came off, then they went to their knees. Roaming hands pulled at zippers and drawstrings, until there were twelve very stiff rods ready to be pleased.

The men enjoyed the tongue and mouth play as the women shared them like a sweet lollipop.

"You the muthafuckin' man," Jay mumbled as he gripped the woman's ponytail and worked her back and forth along his length. His light brown face turned several shades of red as she took him to the back of her throat.

"Enjoy. It's my gift to you." Mason slurred as two dancers sucked and jerked his dick at the same time.

They played with their steel and balls until they were ready to bust, then they strapped them up, turned their backs and slid down onto the pulsating heat. Up and down the women bounced and twerked until the sounds of wet pleasure filled the room.

When their nuts were tender the ladies got up and as if they were playing musical chairs, switched partners, massaged them back to full potential, then bent over the pool table.

The ladies wiggled their plump asses inviting them to come and play. The fearless twelve wasted no time. They stepped behind the ladies almost shoulder to shoulder, slid on new condoms and eased between those soft ass cheeks and deep into those hot wet holes.

The men stroked them against the soft red felt of the pool table as they watched the huge DD's rub against the table as they hit the pussy just right. They fucked them in every way they could switching one hot box for the next.

Jay and Rass sat drunkenly in a booth along the wall.

Mason paid the last of the tips and instructed the cleanup crew. He grabbed a cigar and joined his partners on the couch.

"Damn," Rass exhaled then rubbed his hands over his face.

"Yooooo…you ain't gotta get me another present as long as I live." Rass chimed in.

The men shared a laugh and a few more slick remarks before things got slightly serious.

"I wanted y'all to feel what I felt in Brazil." Mason slurred as he tried to keep his eyes from closing.

Rass shook his head as he re-played the night loudly in his head.

"Man, we are at the top of our game. Fat pockets, good friends, dope ass careers and good pussy." Mason put fire to the end of the cigar.

"Grab a glass," he gestured towards the last three glasses on the tray.

The men reached out, grabbed a shot, and held it in the air.

"Here's to money, power, beautiful women and secret late-night licks."

LATE NIGHT LICK LUST, FEAR, & FIRE

Late Night Early Mornings

Erica looked over at the clock and her eyes squinted when she saw, that is was six o'clock in the morning and she still had not heard from Mason. She reached over, grabbed her phone from between the pillows, and scrolled through her messages.

When she saw she had no alerts, she tossed the phone to the side, and flipped over. She was about to go into a slight panic when she saw his headlights flashing through the window on his way into the garage.

Erica sat up, grabbed her rob from the bottom of the bed, and slipped it on. She walked down the steps and into the kitchen to post up.

Mason fumbled with the locks dropping his keys several times before finally stumbling inside. He tossed his keys on the counter and disarmed the alarm system.

"Oh shit," he yelled as he turned on the light and saw Erica standing there, with her arms folded tight against her chest.

"Don't *'oh shit'* now, I was worried. Why didn't you pick up your phone?" She tilted her head to the side waiting for his side of the truth.

"You know my fraternity brothers are in town. I guess time got away from us." He walked over to where she stood and pulled her into his arms.

"You need to watch your ass. You know you would have a fit if I came stumbling in here drunk as hell, talking about, *'oh my bad, my girls are in town'.*" She stated looking up at him with her lips twisted to the side.

"You right, but can a man have his pussy." He agreed as he began kissing her neck.

Mason didn't wait for a response, he quickly pulled open her robe, pulled her short nighty over her ass, and bent her over the counter. He rubbed up and down her pussy lips until he heard the slippery sound that yelled please enter. He pulled his dick from its enclosure and pushed deep inside her.

"Mas…" she moaned as he began to play between her slippery lips.

Erica was turned on by his aggression. She laid her palms flat on the counter and let him have whatever he wanted.

Mason was on fire, from earlier that night, and he was ready to relive the moment. His mouth watered as he thought about all those big round booties and titties bouncing as they took deep dick.

Erica tensed up, when she felt Mason pull back, and try to force himself in a hole they agreed to never touch.

"Mason, no," she said reaching back to stop his push.

"You said you all mines, right?" He asked as he allowed a little spit to drip from his mouth down the crack of her ass.

"Mason, you promised," Erica pleased as she wiggled against the counter.

"I still promise," he said pinning her hand to her back. "Just relax and let me have what's mine." He replied pushing himself a little further.

Mason gave her short quick thrusts enjoying the tightness of her so-called forbidden place. He released her hand, grabbed her hips and began an easy back and forth stroke.

"Ahhhhh... Mas...baby stop," she panted.

Erica was conflicted. Even though they had agreed to never cross that line. He had stolen her choice.

"Just relax," he whispered as he eased his stroke. "Relax." He repeated as his stomach knotted up with excitement.

Erica moaned and wiggled as he gave her short steady strokes. Just as Erica was about to ask him once again to stop, her pussy began throbbing as his violation began to please her.

"Mas..." she cried, then arched her back to receive more.

Mason's mouth watered as he pushed deeper. He found a steady pace and pumped until he felt her body jerk.

"Right there, baby," she mumbled illegibly. "I'm about to cum Mas'."

"Mmmm...yes...baby cum for me." He fucked faster enjoying his tight wet place.

Mason rode her wave until his toes curled and balls drained. He fell onto Erica's back and sucked gently on her neck.

"Thank you, baby," he said softly while still semi-hard inside her.

"I can't believe I came," she slurred.

"That shit was amazing. I guess I gotta take you out of the country more often." He said as he lifted himself off her weary frame.

Erica turned and watched Mason as he walked away. She pulled herself together, then headed in his direction. She couldn't help but smile as she ascended the staircase.

While Mason thought he was shutting her down, he had actually just opened a door he would never be able to close.

The Workout

"I'm so happy you decided to join me." Leslie said as they entered the gym's locker room.

"I needed that workout. I have been so tensed up."

"Girl it ain't nothing like a good work out or a stiff dick." Leslie laughed as she stepped out of her sneakers.

"Lord why are my friends so crazy." Neena said aloud.

"Somebody gotta be nasty. You always acting all stiff shirt." Leslie chuckled as she pulled her shirt over her brown chiseled frame.

"You never know."

Neena shock her head at the fact of her friend thinking she was still the innocent one in the crew. She just got undressed and headed to the shower.

"Whatever," Leslie said as she grabbed her towel and shower bag, then headed in the same direction.

When Neena returned in her fresh white towel Leslie was already dressed. She turned reached in her locker and pulled her suite from off the hanger.

"I got a call while you were in the shower. I'm going to have to skip lunch mama. I'm sorry," Leslie pouted, walking over to her friend with her arms open wide.

"Like you said whatever." Erica replied as she stepped into her friends embrace.

"See you this time Wednesday." She asked as she hugged Neena.

As Neena got ready to respond she heard a familiar giggle. She looked towards the locker room door and there she was. Neena chocked back her spit as her heat started to race.

"See you Friday." Neena said then put her head down to avoid eye contact.

Leslie turned, grabbed her Gucci duffle and combination lock then headed to the door as she texted her business partner.

"I'll call you mama," she made one last gesture as she exited.

Neena didn't respond out of fear of being heard, instead she watched her move so elegantly in the mirrors. Neena stayed in place until she watched the sexy half naked frame enter the sauna.

Neena grabbed her towel, threw her bag back into the locker, and headed in the woman's direction. She stood at the steamy door watching her as she perched on the wooden bench. She turned the heat down a few degrees, hit the private button, then pulled the glass door open.

"Shhh…" Neena put her finger up to her lip.

Tylinn looked up at her adjusting her vision through the steam.

Neena stood looking at the sweat beading up on her skin. Tylinn realized it was Neena. She didn't know how they ended up in the same room, but she knew it was no mistake.

Tylinn slowly opened her towel exposing her perfectly shaved pussy to Neena who was looking at her like she was ready to eat everything on the table.

Neena opened her towel, threw it on the bench, and walked silently over the Tylinn. It was the moment she had been fantasizing about for months. What were the chances that she would have another chance at tasting this sweet piece of forbidden fruit?

Tylinn eased her hands up and down the lips of her kitty while in full anticipation of what was about to happen. She too had missed the opportunity to spend alone time with the ladies. However, tonight she would not miss any second of their time together.

Neena stepped between Tylinn's legs and kissed her lips lightly. She felt the temperature rise as their nipples connected. She clamped Tylinn's legs to her waste then pulled her kitty right against hers. Their pussies bumped together creating the perfect friction on their clits.

"Sssss…" Tylinn enjoyed the hard grind against her as Neena pushed harder with every movement.

Tylinn grinded slowly against Neena as their tongues played in sync with each other. Neena broke their lip embrace and put her mouth over one of Tylinn's hard nipples.

"Mmmm… I needed to see you," Tylinn moaned as she felt Neena's hand ease between her legs.

Neena didn't respond she was on a mission, she pushed two fingers deep into Tylinn's hot pussy and began fucking her as she licked and sucked all over Tylinn's perfect C cup breasts.

Tylinn moaned and gyrated her hips against Neena's fingers. She gripped the sides of Neena's face and brought her eyes to meet hers.

Neena stared hard into Tylinn's eyes as she enjoyed the pleasure on her face. She played in her wetness increasing the heat between them. Tylinn's legs gripped tighter as she felt the desire to let go.

Neena held their gaze as she sped up her finger stroke. The more Tylinn moaned the more Neena wanted to please her.

"I'm cumming." Tylinn moaned.

Neena took her other hand and circled her clit while pushing inside her even faster. She continued her pussy play, until she felt Tylinn's, muscles grip, then gush her sweetness.

Tylinn fell forward against Neena taking deep breaths as the heat of the room and Neena's desire had her whole body flustered.

Neena proud of her first-time action was ready to see what else she could make Tylinn's body do. She licked her way down between Tylinn's thighs and wasted no time lapping at her pearl.

Tylinn put her head back against the wall and spread her legs wide.

Neena sucked and tickled her clit the same way Sa'Moo had did her. She remembered his every move and copied them. She put her mouth over Tylinn's clit and showed no mercy.

"Oh… My …God!" Tylinn screamed as Neena's tongue circled faster on her clit.

Neena sucked and sucked until, she again felt that warm liquid ease from between her pretty pink pussy lips. She eased her tongue over her pussy lips slowly as she watched her body jerk with every touch.

Neena was in her glory. She ate Tylinn's pussy for over an hour ignoring the knocks and calls from other club members. She had control of the honey and she just wanted it to rain all over her all-night long.

****

Neena smiled and jammed to her favorite songs from Ledisi as she cruised down the highway. She flipped on her blinker and exited on the right, singing and rocking to the beat. She turned each corner feeling the jitters rise in her stomach the closer she got.

Neena was both happy and conflicted. She had broken the rule and to be honest she had no regrets. She briefly reminisced about how the softness of Tylinn's pussy rested against her tongue causing her to crave another taste.

Neena pulled into the garage, closed the windows, then deaded the engine. She stepped out, took in some air, and prepared herself to face Jerome. She battled with should she tell or should she not? They never had secrets, but this was one she needed to keep or at least alter.

"Hey baby," she said leaning over and placing a kiss on his cheek.

"Hey, my love." He returned her greeting looking up at her pretty face.

"I had a crazy long day." She confessed as she came around to take a seat next to Jerome.

Jerome grabbed her legs and placed them on his lap. He carefully removed her shoes and began massaging her feet.

"You want to talk about it?" He looked over at his loving wife.

Neena thought very carefully about her next words then started her story.

"You will never guess who I ran into today." She threw her cards on the table.

"Who?" He asked with a raised brow.

"Tylinn" She paused to gauge his mood.

"Huh? How? Where?" He rattled off questions.

"I got off work and went to the gym with Leslie and there she was." She again paused as she took off her suit jacket.

"Damn, out of all the places on earth. What was she doing there did she say?"

Neena pulled her shirt over her head then continued. "She didn't say much. It was brief. I was so shocked that I didn't really ask to many questions."

"That's crazy as hell." He continued to massage her feet and calves.

"I know. She looked amazing though." She put that on the table, testing his mind set.

"I bet she did. But on the real love. I'm happy we did what we did, but, we have something far more powerful." He turned and looked into her eyes. "I would never want to have to share you. I love you, too much." He confessed easing his hand up her thigh.

"I love you, too." She leaned in and pulled his mouth to hers.

Jerome placed his hands on her waist and lifted her to fit right on top of him. He kissed her widely as she tore at his clothes.

"Fuck me 'Rome," she cried as her body craved to finish what her and Tylinn had started.

Jerome was on fire. He watched as his sexy wife worked her way out of her pants and on top of his stiff dick. She rode fiercely as he breathed heavily while moaning her name.

With each rise and fall against him she hoped to erase the past. She had her taste of the forbidden and now she needed to fuck the rest of the desire out of her system, or so she hoped.

The Forbidden Fruit

"Nah dude, you paying for lunch today." Mason shouted out as he and his colleagues exited the elevator.

"Nah playa. You lost the bet. Minute man ass," Rass joked thinking about how Mason was wiggling while the dancer worked his pipe.

"Sheeiittt…. You saw those vacuum jaws. I'm lucky I even lasted that long." He spoke on the events that took place last night.

The men laughed as they walked down the hall to their office.

"Well count me in for the next one." Tommy said rubbing his hands together.

"We got you." Rass said as he reached his office door.

"Mr. Fitzgerald, I need you in my office real quick." Mr. Steiner yelled out as he walked towards the men.

"Yes sir. Let me throw my things into the office, I'll be right there." Mason walked off.

Mason walked into his office, turned on his computer, then threw his keys and wallet in the top draw. He grabbed his leather note case and day planner and headed to Mr. Steiner's office.

When Mason walked into his boss's office he almost shitted in his pants.

"Have a seat Mason. This is Mr. Conard, he will be financing and heading the next project. I wanted you to meet him before tomorrow's morning announcements.

"Pleased to meet you. I have heard some amazing things about your leadership looking forward to having you work with my team." Sa'Moo said extending his hand.

"Thank you. I enjoyed your portfolio as well." Mason said with a slight crack in his voice.

"I want you to get with Mr. Conard and brief him on the project, then get your team to start an assignment of duties." Mr. Steiner stated his objectives sternly.

"Yes, sir." Mason answered unable to foster any other words.

"Thank you, Paul. I will have my secretary set us up in the big conference room and order dinner. We will be at it for a while." He said with the same stern attitude.

Mason nodded his head. "No problem." He spoke still taken aback that the man they had promised to never see again, was standing right in front of him and now, he was in charge of how he ate.

"Okay then. See you all in the morning. I on the other hand have an appointment." Mr. Steiner said moving towards his golf clubs.

"In the morning." Mason turned to leave the office.

As the door closed Sa'Moo smiled. He had been looking to get deep dick again in Erica's tight pussy and it appeared he had just gotten his way back in.

"What the fuck." Mason mumbled as he closed his office door.

Mason sat hard in his chair and rested his chin on his fist. He sat thinking, what were the odds. How the fuck did a man they met in another country, end up in his office. God had jokes and having Sa'Moo standing in his face showed Karma also had addresses and was at his door ready to serve him his taste of justice.

LATE NIGHT LICK LUST, FEAR, & FIRE

Saturday Afternoon...

"What's wrong you been in your feelings ever since you got home from work last night?" Erica asked, as she seasoned the chicken.

"Nothing, I'm good." Mason responded as he pulled the bags of charcoal out of the kitchen pantry.

"Well you and nothing get it together, because your family will be here all day." She said placing the chicken breast in an aluminum pan.

Mason didn't respond he just walked out of the patio doors and onto the deck.

Erica sucked her teeth and shook her head, as she began seasoning the ribs and shrimp.

Mason stood on the deck conflicted about seeing Sa'Moo. He slammed the coals into the grill and set it ablaze. As the flames started to rise off the black squares, he pondered over how he was going to get around dealing with him. The man he let fuck his wife, was now standing in his reality.

"Mas. Masss..." Erica yelled at the back of his head, as she stood with the heavy pan of ribs.

Mason turned around slow.

"You didn't hear me?" She asked with confusion.

"What's up?" He asked, with a wrinkled brow.

"Look, this is your little cookout. I'm trying to help you." She pushed the tray into his hands. "And your brother just pulled up, he needs help in the driveway." She walked inside slamming the sliding door on her way in.

"Hey sis." Mason's brother Terry said, as he leaned in and kissed Erica on the cheek. "Where you want me to put these?" He asked holding two bags full of dark and white liquor.

"Hey big, brah," she responded forcing a half smile.

"Where my brother at?"

"On the deck," she responded as she returned to the kitchen.

Terry joined Mason on deck. "What's up with shorty?" He asked approaching his brother.

"It's nothing. You need help bringing things in?" Mason responded as he flipped the ribs.

"Yeah some chairs and other shit mommy had me pick up." He responded looking at the tension on his brother's face. He knew something was going on, but he was going to let Mason show his own cards.

Erica moved around the kitchen, as her house began to fill with dozens of guests. She collected purses and platters and put everything in its place. As the hours ticked on and the drinks began to pass, the loud music, laughter and bad family jokes began to wear on her spirit.

"Hey girly, what you up to. You gonna come outside and play cards?" Mason's sister Raynah asked, as she reached into the refrigerator and pulled out a chocolate cake.

"Girl I'm wore out. Y'all go ahead and have fun." Erica responded as she tossed cups and napkins in the trash.

"Come on sis. You gotta have a little fun. You all on your *hazel the maid*, type shit." She chuckled, as she grabbed the paper plates.

"Whatever. I'm about to take a shower. I'll come out there when I get done." Erica said as she cleaned the counters.

Erica watched as her sister-in-law walked out of the kitchen. She then checked on the family in the den and living room, then headed to the shower. Erica quickly slipped into a bright yellow, thin strapped body dress, scented her skin and headed back to her guests.

She walked over and disconnected her cell phone from the charger, then headed to the balcony. The minute she put her foot down on the hardwood, her phone began to vibrate. She walked over to Mason, as she thumbed through her messages and her heart dropped as she read the words.

Erica looked up to catch all four people at the card table staring back at her.

"What's wrong?" Mason asked with a wrinkled brow.

Erica looked up fumbling with different responses, as her heart beat heavy against in her chest.

"I...it's... work." She stumbled with her words.

"What's up?"

"Nothing really, I may have to go in." She recovered as she slid her phone to her side.

Mason looked at her as he picked his cards up off the table.

Erica stood still trying to keep calm, as she planned her next move. Her phone vibrated again, before she could adjust her thoughts. She put a slight smile on her face, walked over to the grill, checked a few pans, then forced small talk at a few tables, as she executed her exit.

Erica slowly pulled the phone to her view, typed in her code and opened the messages.

//: *I need you.*

//: *NOW*

Erica closed her screen, took a deep breath, then eased to the sliding doors and stepped inside. Her eyes scanned the room full of people, as she tried to make it to her bedroom.

Erica closed the door, locked it behind her, opened the messages and typed back.

//: *I don't think I can get away.*

She impatiently waited for the response. When the phone shock in her hands, she quickly opened the message that read.

//: *Baby I need you now. Get in your car and I'ma send you an address.*

Erica's pussy throbbed as she thought about his first touch. It had been months and her body was calling for his heat. She opened a message and got ready to turn down his proposal, just as she began to type her rejection, another text came through.

//: *Hurry I need your pussy on my tongue.*

Erica's fingers shook as she typed without regret.

//: *I'm coming.*

Erica moved to the bathroom, jumped back into the shower, brushed her teeth, and slipped into another tightly fitted sun dress, this time all white with no straps. She scented her skin with Daisy by Marc Jacob, combed through her hair, and painted her lips with a velvet shade of red.

Erica slipped into her high heels, cracked her bedroom door, and peeked down towards the living room. When she heard all the laughter, she eased out the small space, towards the front door. The closer she got to the exit, the harder her heart beat. She stepped out the door and hurried to the car. As soon as she adjusted her seatbelt the phone rang.

"Hello," her voice cracked as she sat waiting to hear his voice.

"Are you in your car?"

"Yes," she said a little over a whisper.

"Good. I can't wait to hold you. Hurry, I need to feel you cum." He firmly stated.

"I'm on my way." She responded feeling like she was in a good dream and a bad nightmare at the same time.

"I just sent you the address. Hurry up and bring me that honey." He responded then disconnected the call.

Erica opened her text, programed her GPS, and headed to where she not only wanted, but needed to be.

Late Night Lick

Erica pulled up to the two-story building and peered out the window. She looked at her phone, then back at the brick-faced dwelling.

"What the fuck are you doing, Erica?" She asked herself loudly, as five-thousand feelings rushed through her body at once.

She rested her forehead on the steering wheel. Her mind went into overload as she thought about the consequences. She battled with throwing the car into drive or run up those steps, into his arms.

Buzz… Buzz…' her phone vibrated against the console.

Erica's head popped up as she fumbled with the screen lock. She punched in her code and read his words.

//: Bring me my gift.

A smile eased across her lips and the fear moved from her heart to her feet, as she forced herself from the vehicle. Erica smoothed her hands over her dress, then walked towards the big red door. She reached out to ring the bell, but the door popped open.

"Welcome." A deep voice spoke to her from the slight crack.

The door opened wider and she stepped into the dimly lit foyer.

"Just go up that staircase." The voice again ordered.

Erica looked up and into the pair of dark brown eyes, as they stared down at her. The man pointed up the stairs and closed the door not breaking his iron-clad glare.

Erica carefully ascended the metal stair case as she looked through the open spaces at the shiny floor below. When she got the top step, her heart sank at the sight of over twenty dozen of white roses. Red and black rose peddles adorned the floor. She stepped into the dimly lit area as the scents caressed her nostrils and the sweet sounds soft R&B played in the distance.

Erica stopped to look at the king-sized bed which appeared to be about four-feet from the floor. There were three sets of steps covered with black fur, surrounding the mattress frame. She looked pass the bed at the floor to ceiling windows between the dark red brick walls.

Erica looked at the city in the distance and smiled as the warm lights glared back at her. She pulled her arms to her chest and crossed them snuggly against her.

"I was waiting for you." Sa'Moo said.

Erica's eyes scanned over to the doorway to see what her dreams had been calling for.

"How did you Fin…" Erica paused as she saw his finger go up to his lips.

Sa'Moo dropped the towel that clung to his waste, then headed over to where she stood.

"Pull your dress down," His deep voice boomed over the music.

Erica slowly slid the top of her dress down, causing her perfect C cups to bounce in their place.

Sa'Moo held her gaze allowing their eyes to communicate what their words could not.

Sa'Moo stepped in front of her with a hard dick and very bad intentions. Erica fought the lump that rose in her throat, he pressed the head of his dick against her clit. Sa'Moo leaned in and kissed her gently on her lips.

Erica's body began to tremble as his muscular frame eased up behind hers.

"I missed you." He confessed moving her hair from her neck.

Sa'Moo eased his hands over her skin and watched as tiny chill bumps rose on her skin. Erica closed her eyes and inhaled, as she felt his soft lips move along the nape of her neck. The cool air erected her nipples as the dress rested on her hips.

The sounds of '*Am I Dreaming*' by *Atlantic Star* caressed her ear drum as Sa'Moo's hands traced along her stomach.

'Things are kind of hazy, And my head's all cloudy inside. And I've heard talk of angels, I never thought I'd have one to call mine.'

"I need you," he whispered.

"I need you too." She responded with labored breath.

"Open your legs," he ordered as he slid his hand over her ass and then between her legs.

Erica replied as soft moans, left her lips. Sa'Moo's fingers forced their way inside her. The music played on speaking her thoughts, as if the artist could read her mind.

Am I dreaming, Am I just imagining you're here win my life,
Am I dreaming.
Pinch me to see if it's real 'cause my mind can't decide

"You know I love wet pussy," Sa'Moo whispered pushing her forward.

Sa'Moo pulled her dress up to her waste and admired her soft round butt, as she rocked back into his fingers.

Erica put her palms against the floor as she felt his dick hardening against her butt cheek. Sa'Moo eased his fingers from their hot, wet place then placed them in his mouth.

"This is what I have been waiting for." He said as he went to his knees.

"Ahhh…" Erica moaned as she felt the tip of his tongue separate her tender pussy lips.

Sa'Moo sunk both hands into her round peach and sucked and tongue fucked her sweat hole. He released one check and reached around to massage her clit.

Erica struggled to hold her stance, as he gave her body what it had been craving.

"Mmmm…" Sa'Moo moaned as he rubbed his lips in her wetness.

"Moooo…" she whined as she felt her body began to quiver.

"Cum in my mouth," he ordered as he pressed harder on her swollen pearl and played in and out of her hole with the tip of his tongue.

When Sa'Moo felt her body jerk, he stood up and slid in. He put his palm on the small of her back, as he broke his way in.

Erica's cries got louder as he fed her inch by inch. When his pelvis began smacking against her thighs he realized there was work that needed to be done and he was ready to clock in. He gripped her hips and pulled her back and forth into him enjoying the slippery sounds her pussy made as he stretched her walls.

"Moo…" she moaned each time his dick touched deep inside her.

Sa'Moo held her firmly in place as he watched her struggle to place her palms to the floor and take all the dick he was throwing.

"Baby faster," she whined feeling her pussy tightening around him.

Sa'Moo gave her exactly what she wanted. He held tight and fucked long and strong. Erica rocked back into the power of his stroke needing to feel those hard inches at her very core. As her juices began to cover him she grinded her waste in a circle so he didn't miss one spot.

"Damn," he hissed as he watched her coat his dick.

"I need to taste you," she purred.

Erica moved forward allowing him to slide out of her, went to her knees and took him to the back of her throat. She worked her jaws back and forth along his inches, swallowing the head with every deep push.

"Mmm…" she moaned as she savored the sweet taste of her pussy on his dick.

"Don't make me come yet baby." Sa'Moo moaned as he pulled her head down on him further.

Erica sucked and moaned as she felt his fingers tighten in her hair. Unable to fight all that good jaw and throat action, he let go. Erica drank all of him, until he began to go limp against her tongue.

Sa'Moo slipped out of her jaw grip, pulled her to her feet, then put her pussy right in his face savoring the taste that his rhythm left behind. Erica rested her legs on his shoulders, put her head back and enjoyed the softness of his lips against hers.

When Sa'Moo saw her stomach tense up he slide her down to fit his waste. Without hesitation he slid right back in. Erica's walls rewarded him, and he took full advantage of having all the control.

"Right there…" Erica panted as he walked her to his bed.

Sa'Moo stopped at the stairs, then laid her against them to hit that pussy from an angle of power. Erica gripped his neck and bit into his chest as he pounded into her.

"We're breaking all the rules," she moaned as his stroke began to erase all her rational thoughts.

"Only rule for good pussy…is to fuck it," he grunted as he climbed into the bed with her trembling beneath him.

"Oh my God." She called out as she felt his pelvis touch hers.

Erica gave up any fight she had left with the next wave of orgasms. She came and cried as he fucked her from one end of the room to the next.

****

5:00 am…

Erica eased off the bed and planted her feet on the cold hardwood. She grabbed the towel from the bottom of the bed and wrapped it tightly around her exhausted frame. She looked over at Sa'Moo who was fast asleep. Erica crept over to where she dropped her hand bag and retrieved her phone.

As Erica entered the bathroom, she closed the door and turned on the faucet. She sat on the toilet and prepared herself for what she knew would be the fight of a lifetime. She entered her code and pulled down the notification bar.

"Damn, twenty missed calls and forty-five messages." She whispered as she opened her text.

Erica's eyes jumped through several,

//: *Where are you?*

//: *Baby please answer your phone?"*

Then, //: *What the fuck is going on?* and //: *What the hell is the matter?*

Erica closed her screen and just rested her head in her hands. As she sat battling with how she should respond. She wanted to be afraid, but fear would not come near her. She was so caught in the moment she was in she wanted to call Mason and tell him she wasn't never coming home.

Erica giggled at the thought, shook her head, then reopened her phone. She stared at the screen contemplating her thoughts then she just let the first thing flow.

//: *I'm fine.*

She hit the send button, then powered off her device. Erica stood removed, her towel, and hopped in the shower. She allowed the water to run over her face as she tried to prepare herself to face the music.

When Erica returned to Sa'Moo's side and eased up next to him and nuzzled her nose in the crease of his neck. Sa'Moo pulled her close to him and breathed her air.

"Thank you, baby. I needed to have you in my arms." He confessed closing his eyes, prepared to doze off.

"Me too." Erica responded as she snuggled even closer. She needed every second to last.

****

When Erica opened her eyes, she glared at the light that beamed in the open space. She sat up pulling the sheet over her breasts. She took a deep breath and prepared her mind to make her ride of shame home. She threw her legs over the edge and rested them on the steps.

"You okay, beautiful?" Sa'Moo asked, as he got to the top of the steps butt naked and sexy.

Erica turned in his direction and with a smile she answered. "Oh, trust me. I'm really good."

"It's like that?" Sa'Moo smiled back.

Erica nodded as he headed to the bed.

"Will I be able to see you again?" He asked as he kneeled before her.

"This is so crazy. I never intended… to…"

"Well I intended to have you." He cut in.

"What about our lives? We are both married. This is crazy." The weight of her decision began to wear on her.

"Don't worry. I will take care of everything. Just rock with me for a little while." He kissed her forehead then headed to the bathroom.

Erica watched as he walked off and his words played in his absence. She looked over at her phone and with hesitation she picked it up and powered it on. Again, there were so many voice and text messages she became overwhelmed with the thought of opening them.

Erica went back and forth with herself before she hit his number and put the phone to her ear.

"Hello," she said with slight fear in her voice.

"Baby, are you okay. What happened? I need you to come home."

"I'm fine, I just needed some time." She responded.

"Look whatever it is. I am ready to talk. No anger, no arguing. We need to sit down and talk." Mason said with pain in his heart.

"We will talk, I will be there in a few."

"In a few? What the fuck is going on?" Mason began to lose his patience.

Erica looked up at Sa'Moo who was now standing directly in front of her. She divided her attention between Mason's elevated voice and Sa'Moo's hard dick.

Sa'Moo stroked himself slowly as he looked down into her eyes. "Open." He whispered.

Erica gave him a sly smirk, then gripped his steel in her hand.

"We can talk when I get home. Just let me get myself together." She said, as she took the head of Sa'Moo's dick into her mouth.

Mason exploded after that nonchalant statement and was now rattling off questions and answering them. Erica tuned him out as she enjoyed all that thickness sliding in and out of her mouth. She sucked and tightened her jaws while he struggled to contain his vocal pleasure.

"Are you listening to me?' Mason's voice boomed through the phone.

Erica pulled back and answered. "Yes. And I will be there to talk about it shortly." She tried to get him off the phone.

Sa'Moo went back to his knees, gripped her legs, threw them over his shoulders, and returned the favor. Erica rubbed the top of his head and he sucked on her clit. She forced one-word answers as she felt his mouth play. Erica laid back and put the phone to the side as tingling sensations moved through her body.

Sa'Moo nibbled her thighs as he rose up between her legs. In one swift motion he slid all the way in not stopping until he hit bottom.

"Ssss…" he hissed as he pulled all the way back and pushed in deep.

Erica covered her mouth trying to stifle her moans. Sa'Moo smiled as he watched her struggle.

"You better let him go before he hears how good his pussy is to me." He whispered in her ear. Then pinned her legs to her ears and picked up his speed.

"I gotta go." Erica panted and ended the call.

The phone vibrated next to her as Sa'Moo stood up in the pussy. Erica held his arms while she watched him slid in and out of her hard and sticky. She laid their thinking if this is the last time she needed to get all he had been waiting to give her.

Sa'Moo stroked deep thinking the same thoughts. He released her legs, cuffed his arms under her shoulder and just fucked her close and slow.

****

Sunday Evening…

By the time the sun was leaving the sky Erica was pulling into her driveway. She deaded her engine, then put her head back as she tried to control her emotions. She looked around at the few cars parked in front of her house and immediately she wanted to put the car in reverse and get back to her sex oasis.

Erica reached for the handle then stepped out. She grabbed her purse from the back seat and headed inside. Before she could touch the door knob she got a text.

//: *Come back.*

//: *I wish I could.*

Erica typed back then turned off her ringer. Her heart beat heavy against her chest bone and her hands began to shake. She tucked the phone in her purse and proceeded inside. As she entered the foyer she heard laughter and music coming from the living room. She took a deep breath, then walked in like she had only made a Walmart trip.

"Good evening," She smiled entering the room.

"Heyyy… my daughter," Mason's mother shouted back as her face lit up with excitement.

"Hey baby." Erica kissed Mason on the lips then walk over to his mother and gave her a big hug.

"We missed you yesterday and this morning." She said kissing Erica's cheeks.

"I'm sorry I had a work project that came up."

Mason's smile turned into a frown as he watched Erica move carelessly in the room. She hugged his two brothers and their wives, then squeezed between them. Mason tried to catch her eye, but she ignored it, putting her attention into everyone else in the room.

When his mother called everyone for dinner, she hurried over to the counter and took a seat. Mason patiently waited stalking her like a lion as the night progressed. When the last plates were packed, and his family piled into their cars, Erica closed the door, set the alarm, then headed upstairs.

Mason checked over the downstairs, cut off the lights, then also headed upstairs to ask the questions he was afraid to get answers to. He walked into the room, he heard the shower running and Erica's Pandora playing along. He glanced over at the nightstand and his eyes settled on her cell phone.

Mason stood contemplating, then without hesitation he walked over and typed in her code. He quickly opened her messages and flipped through them. To his surprise there was nothing but messages from him, his mother, and her assistant. He sat the phone down then headed into the bathroom.

"So, we ain't gonna talk about what happened last night?" He asked staring at her through the glass shower doors.

"What do you want to talk about?" She asked keeping her back turned to him.

"I need to know what is happening with my wife." He stated sternly.

"I needed some time." She gave him short answers.

"I can understand that. But you just going to stay out all night without calling or letting me know you are okay?' His voice escalated.

"I'm fine. I texted and told you I was fine." She responded as she lathered her skin.

"What the fuck are you talking about?" His patience was wearing thin.

·   "Don't raise your voice." She calmly stated as se reached for her towel.

"Look I don't want to fight with you." He reached out and put his hand on her shoulder.

Erica looked up at him and the pain and confusion in his eyes broke her heart. What was she doing? Why was she breaking everything they had built to chase her fantasies?

"Baby everything, I do is for us." He put his other hand on her shoulder. "I'm sorry. Whatever it is, I have said or done. I apologize. I can't never wake up again and you are not next to me." He confessed as the mere thought made him sick to his stomach.

Erica was overwhelmed, she struggled with her words as she saw him fighting to keep the water from rolling down his cheeks.

"We will be fine. I forgive you, baby. And one day I'm going to need you to forgive me." She said a little over a whisper.

Mason pulled her into his embrace. "I love you."

' "I love you too."

Bitter or Sweet

Monday Morning…

Mason exited his car with a crowded mind and heavy heart. One night of swimming in unchartered waters had him feeling like he was drowning in a tea cup of bad decisions. He knew he needed to put an end to his own brand of bullshit and erase any ill feelings he may have had about Erica. They had both crossed lines in their marriage that they never should have, and the recovery process was one he was now focused on.

Mason walked into the lobby of his office building and came to an immediate holt. There were several news stations and photographers scattered throughout the open space. He focused over to the corner where his boss was standing with several men. He walked over and stood a few feet from them as they wrapped up the conversation.

"Here he is, the man of the hour." His boss yelled out as he noticed that Mason was standing there.

"Good Morning." He put his hand up "What's going on here?" Mason asked with a wrinkled brow.

"We just closed two deals with Conard Investment Group. This is a fifty-million-dollar day." He announced and a round of applause followed.

He walked over and put his arm around Mason. "You are the man who brought us the plan that got us the man with the check." He laughed hard and again hands clapped together and cheers rang out.

Mason gave a half smile as the flash from the camera blurred his vision. It was a rise and fall at the same time. He moved in what seemed like slow motion as he realized he had no way out.

They entered the elevator leaving the crowd behind. As the doors shut a limp rose in his throat.

"So, we signed everything except one document and we have to pick up the check." He paused. "He has requested that you work this thing through from start to finish. I trust you Mase. I know you can handle this."

"To be honest. I was going to ask if really this could be put in the hands of Derrick or Tim, they are both very good at what we do." Mason tried to assert his position.

"I won't hear of it." Mr. Steiner mood immediately changed. "Look here Mason. This ain't your momma's grocery money, we're talking eighty million dollars." He huffed looking Mason in the eyes. "This is not just a project. This is my ass, your ass and this companies ass on the line."

The elevator door opened, and Mr. Steiner stepped out. He placed his arm in front of the doors and gave his last demand.

"There is already a meeting set up at Mr. Conards off-site office. Angie will text your phone with the address and instructions. Do whatever it takes to close this fucking deal." He moved his arm and the door began to close. "Whatever it takes Mason."

A barrage of thoughts rushed through Mason's mind as he rode back to the first floor. The elevator doors opened, and he rushed out into the lobby with all eyes on him and his phone vibrating like crazy in his pocket.

As Mason reached the double doors he looked down at his phone, then put it back in his pocket as he made his way to the parking garage. He jumped in his care programmed the GPS then headed downtown.

****

Erica sat giggling at her desk as she went back and forth with Sa'Moo via text. It was now noon and she hadn't gotten any work down between texting, sexting and bullshitting, she was ready for the whole day to be over.

She sat her lunch on the desk, turned on her computer, and tried to get focused when her phone rang.

"Hello,"

"Hey you," Sa'Moo said smoothly.

"You are going to get me in trouble." She turned in her chair.

"I need to see you."

"I'm trying to get off early. But you know it's going to be hard after what I pulled the other night.

"I got something rock hard for you. I'm about to send you my office address. See you soon." He hung up without hearing her response.

Erica sat the phone down and thought about what Mason said this morning about making it right. Then she thought about how good Sa'Moo's dick felt hitting all her spots. She battled for a few seconds then jumped up. She put her lunch back in the bag, grabbed her purse from the bottom drawer then headed to the door.

"I have to do a field report and make some deposits. I will be back in a few." She announced to her secretary looking down at her watch.

She bypassed the elevator and took the steps. She trotted down the eleven flights of stairs fueled by pure animalistic desire.

Erica hopped in her car, turned on the radio and pulled out of her space. As she approached the security desk her phone vibrated in her lap. She hit the navigation then headed to feel the steel.

****

Mason pulled up in front of the four-story building and handed the valet his keys. He walked inside the all glass enclosure and went right up to the desk.

"Yes, he is expecting you," the tiny woman announced with a smile.

Security waved him over and he was checked and escorted to the second floor. Mason's heart raced as he eyed all the security and camera's present.

"Please go in and have a seat." He was instructed, and the door closed behind him.

Mason walked over to the red butter leather couch and took a seat. He sat with his hands together rehearsing his lines. He tried to stay focused, but he kept getting interrupted by the visions of Sa'Moo fucking his wife. He struggled to shake it off, but that shit was at the front of his mind. He needed to do whatever it took to be reassigned from this whole situation.

"Thanks for coming over, this should be quick." Sa'Moo said walking towards where Mason sat. "You can follow me."

Mason stood and followed not to far behind. Sa'Moo opened his office and lead the way inside. He walked over to his large steel desk and slid two documents to the front edge of the desk, then a pen.

"Please have a seat." He offered.

"I prefer to stand." Mason was firm. "Look I believe that my partner Tim will be a better fit for your expectations. I will get the ball rolling, then he can handle you from there. Same service, same company quality." Mason put his offer on the table.

Sa'Moo's mouth formed a smirk, as he realized Mason actually thought he had a choice in the matter.

"I don't think you understand." Sa'Moo said as he pulled out the cigar box and extended it towards Mason.

"No thank you. And yes, I do understand. You want to invest in this company and you need a personal broker to handle all your interest. And I am not it."

Sa'Moo paused then continued. "You are right about my investment. And you're also right about your roll in my interest. However, what you don't understand is this." He stopped, clipped a cigar, and lit the end.

"You don't have a choice. This check." He pointed at the cashiers check that was attached to the contract. "This check right here is your house. Your car…your job…your life." He pulled deeply on the Cuban and blew thick smoke in Mason's direction.

"Excuse me?"

"Oh, you didn't know." He again smirked. "Without you there is no deal." He took another pull. "Without you there is no check."

Mason stood in silence, he glanced down at the check, then back up Sa'Moo.

"Just sign. There is no getting out."

Mason thought about all that he had worked so hard for and all that he had to risk. He slid the pen to the edge of the desk then began thumbing through the pages. Mason signed and initialed each page and when he got to the end he signed next to Sa'Moo's signature, he glanced down at one had seen so many times.

He looked over at the date and his heart dropped to his feet, when he saw the contract was dated back two months ago to the night they had abandoned their vows.

"What the fuck is this?" His eyes jumped up to meet Sa'Moo's smug grin.

"What does it look like?" Sa'Moo responded.

"It looks like my wife's signature."

"Brilliant assessment."

"Why is her name on this contract?"

"She is the seal on the deal." He sat the cigar in the ashtray. Then sat down in his chair.

"What the fuck is going on?"

"You see. She needed something. And you needed something. You get what you want. She gets what she wants." He folded his hands over his chest.

"You crazy as hell if you think you're going to make me fold."

"Listen the deal is done. You get to keep all you have, and you get to share your wife. It's bitter, but its sweet." He responded.

"Does my boss know?" Mason asked as he felt heat running from the top of his head to the bottom of his feet.

"Who do you think sent over the contracts?" He stated not breaking eye contact.

Mason was beyond confused. He thought back to that night, then he thought about the look on his boss's face as he sent him over to basically sign over his wife. Mason was about to go off when the pain driven part of this whole situation rang heavy in his head. *Erica was down.* She had looked him in his face, let him take the blame for all they had been through, and the whole time she was plotting to destroy everything they had built.

Mason put the pen back to the paper and with one stroke signed away everything he loved including his wife.

"Thanks. Security will escort you to your car. Be careful with my money." Sa'Moo said as he sat up to collect the documents.

Mason turned to the door and as he approached, it opened, and security was right there to escort him from the building.

****

Erica pulled up to the address, drove up to the valet and turned over her vehicle. She tugged at her short pencil skirt, as she walked into the building. She stepped up to the front desk announced herself, grabbed a visitor badge and headed to the elevator. When Erica got off she looked around for the number that was written on her pass.

Erica knocked gently on the door and when it popped open a smile eased across her face.

"That's what I love to see." Sa'Moo said pulling Erica into his arms.

"I missed you," she confessed as she felt his arms tighten around her.

"Show me." He whispered in her ear as his hands moved up under her skirt.

Sa'Moo pulled at her thong causing it to drop down around her ankles.

****

Mason washed his hands then ran water over his face. He looked up into the mirror at his reflection and became sick at what he had just become over money and pussy. He reached over, grabbed a paper towel, and headed out the bathroom door.

"You ready?" Security asked him.

"Yeah I'm ready he responded then was lead to the elevator.

As Mason walked behind the tall bald man he thought about the check in his pocket and with each step he tried to say fuck it, but the nagging pain of betrayal stabbed him in the gut.

"Wait right here. I need to sign something real quick." The man said stopping at the desk.

Mason walked over to the wall and posted up and waited. He started to head to the elevator when he heard a light moan coming from Sa'Moo's office. He eased over to the window and peeked through the small space in the blinds.

Mason's eyes widened, and his knees buckled as he watched Sa'Moo slid in and out of Erica. He had her on the edge of the cold metal deck thrusting and grinding. His heart weakened as he watched Erica put her head back and surrender her body to him.

Mason swallowed his spit hard, in an effort not to vomit where he stood. And as if Sa'Moo knew he was watching, he picked her up, fit her to his waist and guided her pussy back and forth into to him inches at a time.

He watched Sa'Moo walk from one spot of the room to the next as she climbed his chest to slow his depth. Her soft breasts bounced, and her nipples hardened as he hit her spots. Mason was caught between pleasure and pain.

Sa'Moo pinned her to the wall right by the window and drilled into her with accurate precision. Erica's light moans mixed with Sa'Moo's grunts vibrating against the wall slightly hardened Masons dick.

"You ready?" Security asked breaking his concentration.

Mason turned slowly towards him and just nodded his head, because he feared what would come out of his mouth. He followed behind the man looking back a few times before he turned the corner.

As Mason took the keys from the valet's hands he took one last look up at the building.

He sat in his seat and as the door shut he said to himself. "Pussy comes with a price or it's free. Either way you get fucked."

He drove into traffic knowing his life as he knew it would never be the same all because he gave in to a Late-Night Lick.

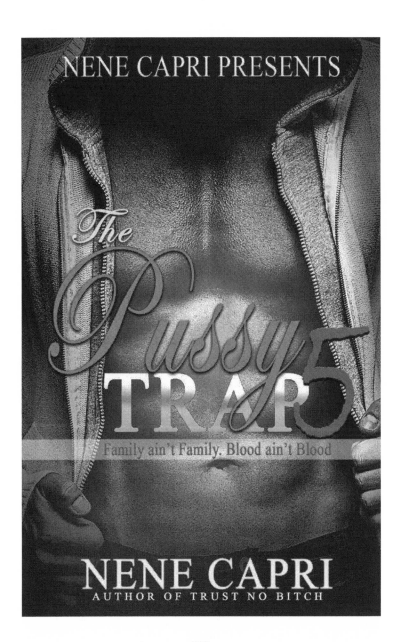

NENE CAPRI PRESENTS

The

Pussy **TRAP 5**

Family ain't Family. Blood ain't Blood

NENE CAPRI

AUTHOR OF TRUST NO BITCH

The Preview

The Pussy Trap 5: Family Ain't Family.

Blood Ain't Blood.

"We gotta do this shit together Mo. It's just me and you. Help me protect our son," he uttered as he picked up speed.

"Ahhhh... daddy," she cried as he hit that spot like only he could.

"Help me Mo," he pulled her legs onto his shoulders and stood up in pussy.

Monique closed her eyes tight as a wave of pleasure took over her mind, body, and spirit. She took in every touch and every taste.

Tyquan closed his eyes and thought about nothing but how good she felt with her legs fearfully clinched to his waist. There he laid in the arms of the only woman who gave him life and with one blink of her pretty eyes could also cause his death.

As their movements took them from one distorted position to another, Monique charged this small amount of pleasure to the fucked-up game they were playing. For Monique pussy was for play, not for power and he surrendered his, the moment he slipped into something hot.

"I wanna ride it daddy," she moaned as he positioned her on top of his throne.

Monique rode slow and easy then placed her feet firm into the bed and bounced to the beat of both of their treachery.

"Get that shit," Tyquan mumbled as he assisted her in her glide pulling her into him hard each time she slid down.

Monique placed her hands on his chest and continued to take all of him with every push. Waves of energy surged through her body as her pussy juices rained down on him.

Tyquan allowed her to bounce until he felt her legs wobble then he let the tables turn.

"Daddy gotta get some now." He teased as he flipped her over and positioned her body to receive him from the back.

Monique looked over her shoulder as she arched her back. "Be gentle daddy," she purred.

"In the morning." He responded stroking his throbbing thickness back and forth until he fit just right.

"Oh my god…" she moaned as the speed and depth of his stroke caused her body to quiver.

Monique dropped her head and rocked into his movements increasing the pleasure for them both. An onslaught of emotions took over and tears formed at the corners of her eyes. Here she was in her enemies' bed enjoying every inch of him. She blocked out all her hate and replaced it with the love to win. They had all chosen the wrong pieces.

Everyone was focused on the king, when in fact, if you move right, the pawn was a king just waiting on his enemies' mistakes.

Tyquan took full control and fucked Monique until she couldn't see a foot in front of her, he laid on her back positioning himself between her soft ass cheeks, then grinded until she begged him to stop.

When he was done making sure her pussy knew who owned it, he came deep inside her womb. Their mouths met, and his tongue danced perfectly with hers'.

"You gonna always be mine," he whispered as he pressed himself firmly against her.

"I know," she uttered as she felt him stiffening inside her.

In Monique's mind, she had a win. In his mind, she had just given a soldier good pussy right before the war. His only hope was that she remained a friend, and not become a major casualty in his war.

NeNe Capri Presents

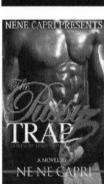
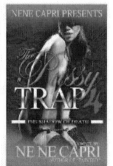

1-CLICK

NENE CAPRI PRESENTS

1-CLICK

 Google Play

Paper backs: Po Box 741581
Riverdale, GA 30274

NENE CAPRI PRESENTS

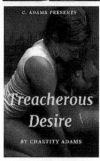

NENE CAPRI PRESENTS

Available in Paperback..!!

The Pussy Trap series 1 -5
Trust No Bitch series 1-3
Tainted 1 & 2
Diamonds Pumps & Glocks
Late Night Lick Vol. 1, 5, 6, 8, 10, 11
By NeNe Capri

Chastity Adams Presents

Gangsta Lovin' 1 & 2
Love Sex & Mayhem 1 & 2
Treacherous Desire
Late Night Lick Vol. 2, 4, 7 & 9
Unsacred Matrimony
By Chastity Adams

We Ship to Prisons:
Po Box 741581
Riverdale, GA 30274

Made in the USA
Middletown, DE
26 June 2021